mys stt 14

The Stork's Surprise

THE STORK'S SURPRISE

Carolyn Greene

Guideposts Books

CARMEL, NEW YORK

www.guideposts.org
(800) 431-2344
Guideposts Books & Inspirational Media Division

Cover and interior design by Cindy LaBreacht
Cover art by Gail W. Guth
Map by Jim Haynes, represented by Creative Freelancers, Inc.
Typeset by Nancy Tardi
Printed in the United States of America

For Kat Jorgensen, a master brainstormer
and awesome friend.
Special thanks to Ting-Po I and David I for help
in selecting the perfect Chinese name.
Thanks to Day Leclaire for offering unique insights.
And a wink and a nod to my "loopy" buddies:
Charlotte Carter, Kristin Eckhardt,
Pam Hanson and Barbara Andrews.

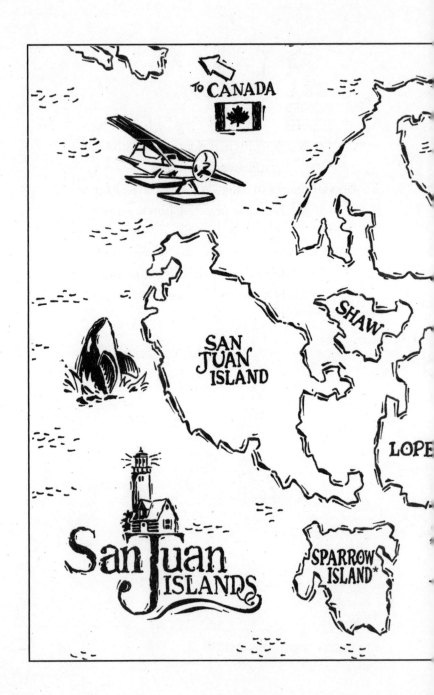

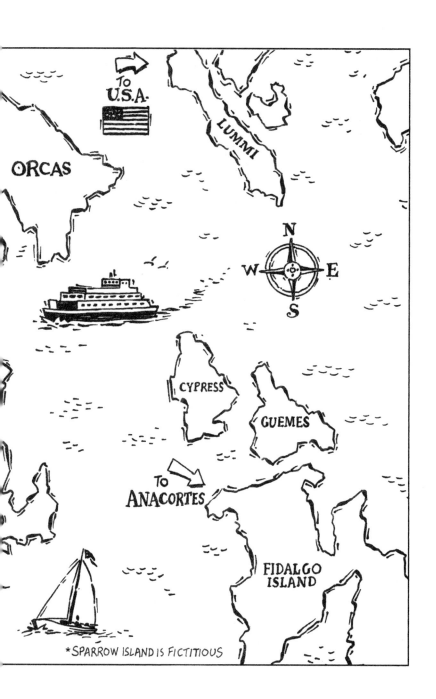

*SPARROW ISLAND IS FICTITIOUS

CHAPTER ❦ ONE

A LADYBUG CAME TO Little Flock Church that warm July morning and performed a crazy flying dance around Abby Stanton's head as she scooted into the pew beside her father.

"You have a friend," said George Stanton as Patricia Hale played quietly on the piano in preparation for the service to begin.

A longtime farmer, Abby's eighty-two-year-old father had taught her to value all of God's creatures, but the black-spotted ladybugs were on his favored list for all the good they did for his crops.

"Could have been worse," he continued as she waved her hand to discourage it from landing on her glasses. "Could have been one of those stinging critters that invited itself in through the open windows."

All the windows that could open in the sanctuary had been lifted to encourage a cross breeze, but the few stirrings of air that had entered the room merely flirted with the idea of cooling the congregants.

Abby's older sister, Mary, maneuvered her wheelchair next to her in her usual place at the end of the pew. Once Mary was settled, she gave her service dog Finnegan a signal that it was okay to lie down beside her and stay off-duty for the duration of the church service.

"Today would be a good day for an air conditioner, wouldn't it?" Mary attempted to fluff up her wilted white curls, to no avail, then just resorted to fanning herself with her bulletin. "Oh well, at least the church still had those extra fans in storage."

Although the temperatures in the San Juan Islands generally remained moderate throughout the year, today was considerably warmer than usual, with the humidity making it feel even worse. The chest-high oscillating fans, stationed at various corners in the sanctuary, hummed like a monotone choir.

Ellen Stanton, seated to the left of her husband, leaned forward to introduce the attractive twenty-something blonde woman on her other side. "Tamara is a volunteer at the Senior Center. This is her first time attending Little Flock Church."

Abby and Mary gave her a warm welcome, as did Martin and Terza Choi, and Joanne Flemming, who had overheard the introduction and turned around to greet her as well.

Tamara Preston was flushed and perspiring. Abby worried that the young woman's heavy frame might be making the heat even more intense for her. Abby prayed that Tamara wouldn't let the temporary absence of a cooling breeze keep her from returning and possibly becoming a member of the church family.

"Her husband travels a lot for work," Abby's mother continued. "Perhaps next time Pete will be able to come too."

Tamara gave a weak smile and waved away the ladybug that was offering its own form of welcome.

In deference to this morning's unusual situation, deacons were passing out paper cups of water to the attendees. Abby snagged a couple and passed them down to the end of the row. It wouldn't do to have a guest dive nose-first to the hundred-year-old plank floor.

Abby watched as her mother took one of the cups for herself and passed the other to Tamara. Although Ellen had been her usual warm, friendly self when making the introductions, something seemed off kilter to Abby...something that couldn't be attributed to the stuffy air.

Abby turned to her sister and said quietly, "It's happening again."

Mary took a deep breath and let it out in a slow, thoughtful sigh. "Yeah. I noticed, too."

Each summer for as long as Abby could recall, their mother had left them for about a week. That was quite a feat considering that while Ellen was gone, her body had stayed on Sparrow Island, doing her chores and going about her usual business. It was her joy that seemed to take a leave of absence.

The piano music grew louder, signaling the congregation to finish their conversations and turn their attention to the front.

After the opening prayer and songs, Abby leaned forward and glanced past her father to sneak another peek at her mother. A faraway expression had taken up residence on Ellen's face.

Normally outgoing, friendly and quick to smile, Ellen Stanton had once again slipped into the gray mood that now blunted her bubbly personality. When Abby had mentioned the yearly pattern to her older sister when they were teenagers, Mary had confirmed she'd also been vaguely aware that something was "off" about their mother's mood. Unfortunately, there was nothing they could do about it. Not when Ellen refused to even acknowledge that anything was bothering her.

Abby's father, a wiry man with lively brown eyes that belied his eighty-two years, smoothly flipped pages in his Bible in search of this week's scripture. The calluses on his work-roughened hands didn't slow him down a bit, and in a matter of seconds the page opened to the tenth chapter of Proverbs and his tanned finger rested on verse nine.

Abby suspected he knew what was burdening her mother's heart. When Abby had been an idealistic teenager who thought she could fix any of the world's problems with a bit of prayer, hard work and a gung-ho attitude, she'd mentioned her concern to her father. But he'd merely said that if her mother didn't want to talk about it, then Abby should respect her privacy.

When George Stanton offered advice, people usually followed it. Abby had been no exception. But that didn't stop her from caring.

Or wondering.

Noticing her looking in his direction, George shifted the book to his right knee so that Abby could read along as Rev. Hale recited the verse aloud.

"The man of integrity walks securely, but he who takes crooked paths will be found out."

Abby smiled as she remembered the Bible drill tips her father had taught her when she was a child. All of the *T*s— Thessalonians, Timothy and Titus—were clustered in alphabetical order together near the back of the Bible. And Psalms and Proverbs—the books of worship and wisdom—could be found at the center of the Bible, just as the very values they taught were best found at the center of people's lives.

Abby settled back on the worn wooden pew and fanned herself with the bulletin.

On the row in front of them, a tangle of dark curls bobbed just above the top edge of the pew as three-year-old Beau squirmed beside his foster mother. Joanne Flemming laid a calming hand on his shoulder, and the child's wiggling reduced to mere foot swinging, as evidenced by the gentle rhythmic thumps that followed.

Rev. Hale stepped out from behind the lectern and walked up the aisle as he continued the sermon, his heels clicking on the hardwood floor. He paused occasionally to catch the eyes of the young members of the Skills and Crafts program.

"Competition can bring out the best—or the worst—in people," he said, making it seem as though he was speaking to each of them individually.

When the handsome forty-five-year-old pastor had first come to Little Flock, some of the members were taken aback by his occasional creative approaches to delivering his message. But eventually they came to see that there was no grandstanding on his part . . . just a sincere desire to reach the congregation and plant the word of God in their hearts.

"The Skills and Crafts group is extending brotherly love to a church on the mainland, trying to raise money to help those children start their own group. As you go into this competition, God wants you to walk with integrity." He paced the length of the aisle as if demonstrating in his tall, upright posture how they should conduct themselves. "Focus on helping as well as winning, and ask God to walk with you and to keep you away from the crooked paths."

Abby had to hand it to Rev. Hale for keeping things so

interesting that no one dozed off in the heat. Throughout the church, though, men dabbed their faces with handkerchiefs.

Beside her, Mary flapped the neckline of her strawberry-print blouse. Although her movements were loose and relaxed, her mouth was not. While the pastor returned to the lectern to finish his sermon, Mary's thoughts clearly weren't following him.

The ladybug returned and landed on Abby's wrist. She'd heard the saying that it was bad luck to kill a ladybug, but that wasn't what drove her to try to capture the insect in her folded bulletin. She never killed anything if she could help it. Today this rascal would be going back outside where it could make itself useful.

While she was attempting to scoop it up in the folds of the paper to transfer it to her empty water cup, Abby accidentally flicked the creature to the pew in front of her where it entertained little Beau with its erratic flight. When it settled on the back of the pew, Beau scrambled to his feet and leaned his tummy against the seat back, his cleft lip curled in delight as he watched it crawl onto his foster mother's shoulder.

Unaware of what was going on, Joanne curled an arm around his little waist. Since he was being calm she let him stand there, quietly entertaining himself.

The tiny bug continued to crawl, moving past Joanne's collar and sure-footedly making its way up a strand of her shoulder-length sandy brown hair. Thoroughly amused, Beau let loose with a little giggle. Joanne casually laid her free hand on his back and patted him as a gentle reminder to save the giggles for later.

The last thing Abby wanted was to distract a fellow parishioner during church. But neither did she think it right to just sit and watch the creature invade her friend's hairdo. Slowly, casually, Abby leaned forward and lifted a finger to encourage the red-and-black adventurer to climb aboard.

Joanne lifted her hand from Beau's back and flipped her hair, sending the hitchhiker flying once more. This time it circled quickly and landed on the knuckle of Beau's thumb.

A delighted cackle rang out over the hum of the fans. With a movement so fast that only a stop-action movie camera could have caught what happened, Beau popped the little crawler into his mouth.

Then, turning to Abby, he flashed her a smile so endearing she almost thought she'd imagined that he had suddenly become an insectivore.

AS THEY EXITED THE CHURCH, Joanne and Beau were waiting for them on the small portico.

Joanne didn't look like a grandmother in her early sixties. With an athletic build and only a few barely noticeable sprinkles of gray in her light brown hair, she could have easily passed for someone in her late forties. She also had the energy of a much younger woman, which was a good thing since lately she was using it all up on Beau.

"I want to thank you for your quick actions," Joanne said, addressing Abby. "He didn't draw blood, did he?"

Abby opened her hand and lifted her palm upward. After only a second or two, the ladybug—rescued and now dry after an inadvertent exploration of Beau's mouth—caught a light current and ferried itself to a rhododendron bush beneath the church windows.

She flexed her index finger and held it out for Joanne to see. "Just a little dent in the skin. Those baby teeth are sharp, but there's no harm done."

Mary set the brake on her chair and laughed as she recalled what had happened. "I haven't seen you move that fast since we were kids."

"I'm just glad you did," Joanne said. "Who knows what kind of trouble it might have caused if he had choked on the ladybug."

While the women considered the possibilities, George reached for Finnegan's leash to take him for a short walk. Ellen stayed behind, but she still wasn't saying much.

Abby was concerned about her sister as well, but now was not the time to broach the subject. Perhaps whatever was on her mind would come tumbling out later when they were relaxing or just puttering around the house. Abby often found that doing the dishes or getting ready for bed were the best times for talking about subjects that were difficult to get started.

"He may be with me for a while longer," Joanne said, squeezing the child's hand. "When adoptive parents hear about the work that's left to be done on the palate, they lose interest and start looking elsewhere."

Beau paid no attention to their conversation, preferring instead to pull on Joanne's arm and point at Finnegan, who was walking with George along the edge of the church property.

Abby was touched by Joanne's concern for little ones who needed a temporary family. A few years ago, when a social worker had spoken to Little Flock Church about the need for emergency and long-term foster families, Joanne and her husband—along with Ellen and two other members—had been moved to go through the certification process. On one occasion, a seven-year-old girl had been placed with Ellen for a couple of hours after she was accidentally separated from her parents who were vacationing on Sparrow Island. The reunion had been heartwarming, and Ellen still treasured having been able to help a family in their time of trouble.

The Flemmings, however, had extended their training so that they could help for longer than the two weeks authorized by the state's child welfare system for short-term emergency care. Although Beau was happy enough with Joanne and Clint, they were not in a position to take on the permanent responsibility of raising him.

From the rear of the church, Martin and Terza Choi waved a friendly good-bye as they headed toward their car. Joanne, Mary, Ellen and Abby all returned the gesture.

"I'd like to see him get started on the adoption process before he has his next surgery." Joanne braced herself against the boy's repeated tugging. "It's hard for a little one to go through that kind of medical procedure when it's uncertain which family he'll be staying with next."

Mary cleared her throat. "We'll pray for a wonderful adoptive family for him. A family that has plenty of love to share."

"Yes, of course," Abby agreed. She made a mental note to put Beau at the top of her prayer list.

With a final mighty tug, the little boy broke loose from Joanne's grasp and darted toward the parking lot.

Mary swung an arm out as he dashed past her chair, but he deftly circumvented her grasp. Then he zoomed past Abby and Joanne and bolted into the parking lot toward Finnegan, yelling, "Doggie! Doggie!"

Although most of the cars had departed by now, a few were still leaving. Abby's worst fear was that someone might come around the blind curve at the back of the church and not see the little boy with the single-minded goal of petting the dog.

She could see the concern in her father's eyes as he watched the little boy with the big personality come tearing across the parking lot like a rabbit with a fox on his tail, but there was no way George could reach Beau quickly from that distance.

As one, Abby, Ellen and Joanne took off, and Mary followed pushing her wheelchair down the ramp after them. Abby's flat-heeled shoes gave her the advantage, and she was vaguely aware that the others had quickly dropped back. From across the way, George gave a shout as Finnegan, sensing trouble with the toddler on the loose, half-dragged George toward the little curly-haired whirlwind.

A car's engine turned over just around the corner. Abby's heart raced, but somehow she managed to squeeze out a prayer as she forced her legs to churn faster. *Please, God, let one of us reach him before a car comes around that corner!*

Martin, ever the gentleman, had been opening the passenger door for his wife when the ruckus started a mere fraction of a second earlier. As soon as he saw what was happening, he did something that was thoroughly un-Martin-like: He left Terza standing by the car. Then he ran toward the boy, his straight, black hair flopping against his forehead.

In just a few strides Martin closed most of the distance between them. Beau disappeared around the bend with Martin right on his heels.

Abby started to breathe again, relief slowing her steps, when the loud thud of flesh against steel reverberated through the heavy mid-day air.

Joanne's scream split right through Abby's heart, then plummeted to the pit of her stomach.

The compact car's front end jutted out from behind the

building, but the bushes blocked her view. As best she could tell, both Martin and Beau were on the ground.

Steve Hunsicker, a man in his early thirties, had got out of his car and now sprinted to the pair in front of his bumper. He and his wife Jenny knelt beside the pair.

Bile rose into the back of Abby's throat, and she feared she might be sick. But her concern for the child overrode her body's natural reaction to the shock of hearing the collision. She tried not to imagine the potential harm that could have come to either or both of them, but just kept reminding herself, *God is in control. God is in control.* The thought was amazingly comforting.

Even so, Abby wasn't about to just sit back and wait to see what God did with the situation. With a renewed burst of energy, she picked up her speed. Joanne was right behind her, screaming Beau's name.

As they approached the scene of the accident, Abby attempted to position herself between the boy and Joanne.

At that moment, Martin rose from in front of the car, the boy in his arms. Gently, he smoothed the child's clothing with the palm of his hand while clutching him securely against one hip.

Beau, impervious to the fright he'd given everyone within range of Joanne's screams, leaned over and laughed as Finnegan danced in circles around Martin's legs in an attempt to sniff the boy and ascertain that he was all right. The dog's leash trailed behind him.

Everyone gathered around. George retrieved Finnegan's leash and led him to Mary who, by now, had pushed her way along the sidewalk to where the commotion had happened.

"I'm so sorry, I'm so sorry," the driver repeated to everyone who would listen as his wife clung to his arm. "I didn't see him."

It seemed evident by Beau's wiggling that he had come through the incident unscathed, but Abby was worried about Martin. Other than having a bit of dust on the knees of his trousers, he seemed fine physically. But his golden, tanned face had paled to a sallow hue.

By now, Terza was by her husband's side, fussing over him and the child. She ran her hands over Beau's face, peering into his eyes as she did so. Then she gently stroked the boy's arms, chest, tummy and legs. Abby stepped aside to make room for Joanne who moved next to her and watched with interest. The only time Beau flinched was when Terza's slim fingers brushed too close under his arms. With a bubbly giggle, he clapped his elbows to his sides, ducked his head and hunched over to ward off any more inadvertent tickles.

After Martin hugged the boy and handed him off to Joanne, Terza pulled her husband aside and quietly spoke to him in Chinese. She seemed as shaken as he was, but her concern was for him.

Martin replied to her in their native language, his voice soft and soothing. Abby didn't need to understand Chinese to know that their strong reaction to the incident was about more than just what had happened in the past moment.

The couple, still only in their mid-fifties, had already lived a life more full than most people their age. Though they never spoke of it, Abby had heard that they'd lost their only child many years ago, but no one knew any details of how it had happened.

"Mr. Choi, I'm so sorry." Steve shifted his weight from one

foot to the next and repeatedly wrung his hands. "When I heard that loud thump—"

"God is good," said Martin. "The little boy, he is fine." He smiled and lightly smacked the car hood with the flat of his hand. "Small cars make big sounds," he added, letting them know that he had hit the automobile as a warning to the driver.

Joanne jostled Beau on her hip. When he wriggled to get down, she held him tighter. "Thank you, Martin. Thank *all* of you."

The group huddled together for a few more minutes, exclaiming over the near accident and eyeing both Beau and Martin to make sure there were no heretofore unnoticed injuries. As they gathered and recovered from the shock, George offered a brief but heartfelt prayer of thanks to God for sparing the child from injury or even death.

Martin grasped his wife's hand and gave a squeeze. "We need to get back to The Bird Nest and take care of your birders," he said to Abby. "They say you'll be taking them out at the crack of dawn tomorrow."

A graduate of Cornell University with a PhD in ornithology, Abby had spent thirty-five years in New York, studying the feathered creatures that had fascinated her all her life. After the automobile accident that had left her sister in a wheelchair, Abby had returned home to Sparrow Island. She now worked as the Associate Curator at the Sparrow Island Nature Conservatory and occasionally led bird-watching expeditions for small groups of tourists. This particular group—most of whom were staying at the Chois' bed-and-breakfast—was scheduled for daily bird-watching tours on various parts of the island for the next couple of weeks.

Bird-watching was one of Abby's favorite activities, and it only got better when she was accompanied by fellow enthusiasts. Occasionally, the bird-watchers brought tagalongs—friends or family members—who were reluctant sidekicks. Mary had once jokingly referred to the non-enthusiasts as "dragalongs." Abby, however, enjoyed exposing the neophytes to the subject she loved most.

This group, however, had no dragalongs since the ten-day commitment had weeded out all but the most devoted birders. Jenny Hunsicker and a college friend from the mainland who was due to arrive today had also signed up for the excursion.

"Yes, we'll need to be in our places before the birds become active," Abby said, "but that should leave plenty of the rest of the day for them to explore the shops and play tourist."

Eager to be on their way after the heart-stopping event, the adults waved "bye-bye" to Beau as they retreated to their respective cars.

It wasn't until George had turned Mary's chair to rejoin Ellen that Abby realized her mother had remained frozen in the spot they'd left her when everyone had taken off running toward Beau.

As they drew closer, Abby saw that her blue irises seemed even bluer in contrast with the red that rimmed her eyes.

Ellen sniffed self-consciously and averted her head as she used the heel of her hand to wipe away the moisture that glistened in her lashes.

It wasn't just the tears that caught Abby's attention. That was perfectly understandable. In fact, Abby had been close to tears herself when she'd thought Beau or Martin had been struck by the car. Even now, her heart still pounded in response to the fright.

But it was the stricken expression on her mother's face that concerned Abby. It was as if she was in shock. Ellen wasn't the type to fall apart during a crisis—not even when Abby and Mary had been roughed up and scuffed as kids. Even her response to Mary's paralyzing accident had been somehow different from this, so Abby wasn't sure what to make of her unusual reaction.

George released his grip on Mary's chair and went to his wife. Putting an arm around her shoulders, he said to the two of them, "We're going home now. I'm sure we'll both feel better after a nice lunch."

Mary turned and caught Abby's eye as their parents went to their car.

"What do you make of that?" Mary asked.

"I don't know," said Abby. "But the incident with Beau seems to have triggered some very intense emotions."

OUTSIDE THE SENIOR CENTER the next morning, Ellen gathered her supplies and let herself out the passenger side of the big Lincoln. Samuel Arbogast, the hired hand who helped George keep the farm running, reached for his door handle.

"You don't need to get out," Ellen told him. "There's not that much for me to carry." She lifted the canvas tote filled with recipes and cookbooks to show that she could handle it by herself. A container of lemon meringue mini tartlets perched atop the contents. "Thanks for the ride."

The Lincoln belonged to Ellen who, at eighty years of age, could still drive. However, at this stage of her life she felt more comfortable letting others maneuver the big vehicle through the narrow streets of quaint little Green Harbor.

This morning, Sam had generously offered to drive her to

the Senior Center for some crafts and socializing. Ellen needed to stay busy, especially now, and socializing with her friends helped distract her from the feeling of unease that settled over her at this time every year.

For today's project, the seniors were to bring their favorite recipes to share with the others. Sampling each others' dishes was part of the fun.

Sam remained behind the wheel and peered toward the Senior Center building. A crease furrowed between his eyebrows.

"It doesn't look like anyone's here yet," he said through the open passenger-side window.

Since today's project had been her idea, Ellen had felt it was only right to arrive early and start setting the supplies out for the crafters. She had already brought a batch of her favorite magazines last week and left them here for her friends to use in searching for new recipes. Some of the others had been instructed to bring markers and index cards along with their own recipe boxes and annotated cookbooks.

"It's okay. I have a key," Ellen said with a smile as she fished it out of her purse.

"I'll wait until you're in."

Ellen appreciated Sam's concern. When he was younger, he'd fallen into a life of crime, committing petty larcenies and breaking and entering, which landed him in the state prison at Walla Walla. Eventually, he'd found God, which led to a change of heart and ultimately a change in his life. In his early forties, when Sam was released from prison and no one would give him a chance to start over, George and Ellen had hired him to work on the farm. In the more than ten years that he'd been with the Stantons, they had never regretted their decision and Sam had never forgotten their kindness. But his devotion to the couple sometimes led him to be a bit overprotective.

Today was one of those days.

"I'll be fine. Emma Stoltz and the others will be along in a few minutes."

Just as she had anticipated, Sam's sense of responsibility to the farm and its animals overrode his need to hover over her. "Call me when you're done, and I'll be back to pick you up."

"Thanks, but Emma said she'd give me a ride home."

Sam smiled and waved, his teeth bright against his sun-darkened skin.

As the car pulled away, Ellen hitched her purse strap up over her shoulder. She tightened her grip on the tote handle and separated the Senior Center key from the others on her key ring.

Ellen looked down, stepping carefully over the brick path through which a few tenacious blades of grass sprouted. From somewhere nearby, perhaps at the post office next door or even the bank beyond that, a rustling sound disturbed the misty morning haze.

Ellen paused and turned in the direction from which she thought the noise came, but saw nothing. Perhaps it was a postal worker preparing the mail for today's deliveries, she told herself. Although Abby had been out since dawn with her birding group, most of the shopkeepers in Green Harbor were only beginning to flip the signs in their windows to "Open" and prepare their businesses for the day ahead.

Bypassing the wheelchair ramp, Ellen took the steps up to the small porch. There, on the welcome mat in front of the door, sat a handwoven basket with a blue print bow on the handle. Matching fabric lined the basket.

Ellen frowned. Today's recipe-swap project had been announced last week. Although the group had agreed that each member would bring his or her favorite dish to share with the others, no one was required to do so. Perhaps someone needed to skip today's meeting and decided to leave their culinary offering for the others to enjoy.

"How thoughtful," Ellen said to herself as she spied a card pinned to the cloth that covered the contents of the basket.

Wondering which of her friends might have had to miss the meeting, Ellen set her tote bag on the porch as she reached for the note.

Just as her fingers closed around the card, something beneath the cloth moved.

Ellen straightened and clutched her chest. In a strange slow-motion sequence, she instinctively backed away from the unexpected surprise. As she did so, her foot caught the edge of the top step, her heel hanging over in mid-air.

Off balance, Ellen swung her arms to right herself. As her weight shifted backward, she uttered a fervent prayer. "Lord, please don't let me break a hip!"

CHAPTER ❦ TWO

ABBY WALKED INTO THE kitchen, still fresh from her shower. The bird-watching tour had gone well this Monday morning, and no one had missed their predawn appointment to gather for the van ride.

For that, she had Terza Choi to thank. Between the alarm clocks provided at the inn and Terza's polite knocks on her guests' doors, none of the bird enthusiasts had slept through the first morning of their ten-day birding tour. To Terza's way of thinking, the more her guests enjoyed themselves on the island, the more likely they were to come back to stay at The Bird Nest during future vacations.

"You look nice and perky," Mary said from her seat at the kitchen table. She was making sandwiches, and two brown paper bags lay on the table nearby. Since Finnegan had not yet been dressed in his work cape, he took his time eating a leisurely breakfast of dog food topped with a small leftover portion of scrambled egg. "Did you spot a dodo bird or maybe an ivory billed woodpecker?"

Abby grinned at her sister. Mary knew as well as she that the former was extinct and the latter had been declared extinct in the fifties and was only recently reputed to have been seen in a different part of the country. Neither, of course, would have been a typical specimen in the San Juan Islands.

"No, but we did see some Guillemot pigeons and a fox. You would have loved the stonecrop blooms." Abby picked up the apples Mary had set out and took them over to the sink for a scrubbing.

Mary spread mustard on the bread. "Considering how much sand and mud you brought back on your hiking shoes, you must have led your group all over Sparrow Island."

"No, just to the 'breakfast bar' at Paradise Cove," Abby said, making a joking reference to the number of shorebirds that frequented the cove in search of food in the quiet waters. "We'll go over toward Mount Ortiz later this afternoon and look for eagles. Wayfarer Point is on the schedule for tomorrow."

In the bird-watching groups she led, there were usually one or two people who were infatuated enough with the feathered creatures to go off on their own afterward and continue their observations. But most were hobbyists who came to the San Juans for the express purpose of combining birding with the assorted touristy activities offered on the islands. Abby supposed a few of the birders might opt for a relaxing nap on the beach this afternoon. She didn't have time for such a luxury herself since paperwork and other duties awaited her at the conservatory. Fortunately, none of those duties were of an overly urgent nature.

She buffed the apples with a towel, then placed them in the paper bags and sat down beside her sister. "It's interesting how, when one bird in a flock is uneasy, the rest of them pick up on the tension."

"Yes, what a blessing that God gave such sensitivities to all His creatures." Mary cut the sandwiches in half diagonally. Then, her fingers shaking slightly, she cut them in half again.

"He gives them that ability as a way to protect the whole flock. If one is disturbed about something, that bird's unrest also affects all the others."

Mary didn't meet Abby's gaze. Instead, she held the knife over the sandwich portions as if trying to decide whether to remove the crusts. "Was something bothering your birds this morning?"

"No, not the birds." Abby ripped off two pieces of wax paper and placed them on the table. She watched while Mary set the knife down and turned her nervous energy to wrapping them. "How about you?"

Mary sighed and abandoned her efforts at lunchmaking. "Me? I'm okay. I'm just concerned about Bobby."

"What, is he sick?"

Their neighbor's ten-year-old son was a frequent visitor to their house, often staying with Mary after school while his mother finished up her teaching responsibilities at Green Harbor Public School. The precocious little boy was like an honorary family member to all the Stantons, so they all naturally kept tabs on him.

"No, it's his attitude. When I spoke with him yesterday about the walkathon, he only seemed concerned about winning the prize for soliciting the most sponsors." She leaned back in her chair and rested an elbow on the padded arm. "He's being so competitive, I'm afraid he's losing sight of the purpose behind the fundraiser."

Mary finally met her gaze, but Abby could tell that it wasn't only Bobby's attitude that was bothering her sister. Something else had settled heavily on her heart. Mary was usually pretty good about expressing whatever might be bothering her, so Abby found her hedging disconcerting.

"What else is going on, Mary?"

"Well . . ." She gripped the chair arm, her knuckles turning white. "Let's just drop it. I don't want to stir up a fuss."

Abby frowned, recalling her sister's surprise and distress over Rev. Hale's announcement in church yesterday. And then it hit her. "You weren't included in the planning for the walkathon, were you?"

Mary waved a hand to bring an end to her questioning. "Don't worry about it."

As if sensing a change in his mistress's mood, Finnegan left the rest of the food in his dish and padded across the room to Mary. Habit prompted her to ruffle his ears, and the dog seemed to smile his pleasure.

"I'll be fine," Mary insisted.

Abby had no doubt of that. Her sister was no shrinking violet, as evidenced by the strength she'd shown when recovering from the car accident. And she continued to be strong in her adjustment to her new lifestyle, never complaining about her limitations, but only seeking to live a life that was as fully normal as her circumstances would allow.

Mary thrived because her relationship with God had allowed her to move on from the shock of the news the doctors had given her. Her faith, though temporarily shaken, had never been lost, and it was stronger now than ever before. So why was she so reluctant to say what was on her mind?

And then Abby knew. Although Mary had recovered from the accident, not everyone else had. In their loving concern, sometimes friends tried to shield Mary from reminders of the trauma she'd been through.

"That's it. You weren't asked to help with the walkathon."

Mary released a pent-up breath, the air escaping her lungs with a soft hiss. "I'm sure they meant well."

"Of course they did. But that doesn't mean it doesn't need fixing."

"Leave it be, Abby."

"Is that what you said when Thelma acted weird about asking Nana to join us for the gospel group that performed at the church last winter?"

Just over a hundred years old and the oldest actively attending member, Sarah Freewater was known to everyone in the congregation as "Nana." Her hearing had recently failed her, but her spirit remained indomitable. Though she couldn't hear what the pastor said as he delivered his sermons, he provided her with a copy of his sermon notes and somehow she knew exactly when to turn to her Bible or laugh at his jokes. Never once had she asked for concessions because of her deafness.

Mary pushed a white curl away from her forehead, then smoothed the rest in place. "Thelma was trying so hard to be sensitive that she almost cut Nana out of the fun."

Abby nodded her understanding. "All because she couldn't bring herself to ask if Nana wanted to come 'listen' to the concert." She laughed as she recalled the elderly woman's solution to the problem.

Mary's expression relaxed. "I've never heard one person use the words *listen, hear* and *sound* so many times in one short conversation. After Thelma realized what Nana was doing, she got over being so uptight about her situation."

And now the same thing was happening to Mary. Only, this time the leaders of the Skills and Crafts program were being uptight about involving her in the walkathon.

"Perhaps we need another lesson in overcoming stereotypes," Abby suggested. When it seemed as though her sister was about to put up resistance, she reminded her, "They won't know if you don't tell them. Besides, Nana didn't need to raise a fuss to get her point across. Neither do you."

In Nana's case, they'd all been delighted to discover the elderly woman tapping her orthopedic shoes to the rhythm of the gospel tunes. Though she couldn't hear the music with her ears, she could hear it in her heart as the vibrations stirred her recollections of the old-time favorites.

A long pause followed her statement. Abby knew that her sister wasn't ignoring her. She was just thinking it over.

Mary dropped the wrapped sandwiches into the lunch bags and handed one to Abby. "I'll be going to Island Blooms today to help Candace with some flower arrangements, but I should be back in time to fix dinner. Will you be back from your birding in time for some homemade tetrazzini?"

"That sounds good. Thanks." Abby also expected that Mary would have made up her mind what to do by then.

On the counter, Abby's purse began playing the tune to *Mama Mia*.

As she retrieved the cell phone, Mary moved away from the table. "I wonder why Mom's calling. She said yesterday that Sam had agreed to take her to the Senior Center this morning."

Abby shook her head and lifted her shoulders as she flipped

the phone open. "Maybe she forgot one of her favorite recipes and wants me to bring it to her."

The tone of Ellen's voice told Abby it was about something more crucial than a recipe.

"Mom, are you okay?"

Mary and Finnegan both stopped at the door to the living room and watched intently as she strained to hear what was being said. "I'll be right there."

When she hung up the phone, Mary asked, "Is something wrong? Do you want me to come with you?"

"No, I don't think that's necessary. She just said she found something unusual at the Senior Center and wants me to come take a look." Abby picked up her purse and slung the straps over her shoulder. "I'll call you later and let you know what it's all about."

"WHAT TOOK YOU SO LONG?"

Abby hadn't even pulled to a complete stop when her mother grabbed the car door handle to open it.

Ellen didn't wait for an answer. "Come over here," she said, leading the way across the front lawn. "I wouldn't have believed it myself if I hadn't seen it with my own eyes. Shocked me so bad I almost fell backward off the porch. It was a good thing I'd been practicing those Pilates exercises. Otherwise, I would have never been able to catch my balance."

As Abby approached the porch, Ellen moved in front of her and led the way inside to where a decorative basket sat on the craft table.

"I found this on the porch. Careful, don't drop it," she said, placing the basket in Abby's arms.

Once Abby had a secure grip on the basket, Ellen pulled back the blue cloth.

Two of the darkest brown eyes Abby had ever seen stared back at her. "Goodness gracious. Lord, have mercy," she whispered.

The newborn closed its eyes and drifted back to sleep. The round cheeks wrinkled as it made small sucking motions with its lips.

"It's a baby," Ellen declared quite unnecessarily. "Somebody just left it there on the doorstep. As soon as I realized what it was, I called you."

Wisps of fine black hair peeked out from under the home-made handkerchief bonnet that covered the infant's head. The child's pink cheeks were still blotchy from its recent birth.

Abby pushed back the beach towel the baby had been wrapped in, and its tiny fingers curled reflexively as its free arm swung outward. Instead of a diaper, a green linen kitchen towel was held together with a couple of strips of duct tape. A plastic grocery bag with leg holes cut in it was fastened over the makeshift diaper. Carefully, so as not to disturb the sleeping child, Abby loosened the tape and peeked inside.

"A boy," she said, "and he's still dry. Someone must have left him here only minutes before you arrived."

"It's like Moses," Ellen said reverently, "only this baby wasn't hidden among the bulrushes and we're not the pharaoh's daughter."

Abby turned and looked around, half expecting to find the baby's older sibling lurking nearby, just as Miriam had done in the Bible. But the post office to their right showed no sign of anyone outside, and the bank beyond it remained dark. To their left, the shuffleboard and badminton courts sat empty beneath hovering shrouds of early morning mist.

"Did you see anyone hanging around when you arrived this morning?"

"Not a soul," said Ellen. "I thought about what you would have done if you were here, so I walked to either side of the building to see if anyone was hanging around. I thought I had heard a noise in the bushes over there, but when I didn't see anyone, I just assumed it was a bird or small animal scuttling among the branches. Whoever left this baby was gone by the time I discovered the basket."

Ellen reached into the basket and withdrew a small card.

"This is a clue, but it doesn't tell us much."

Without releasing her grip on the basket in her arms, Abby leaned closer to read the card her mother had opened.

"I've done a very bad thing. I can't give my baby the kind of family he deserves. Please take care of him and tell him his mother loves him very much."

The message had been printed in block letters to disguise the handwriting. As for the paper it was written on, the plain white stationery gave no indication of who might have penned the note.

The baby squirmed in his tiny bed and whimpered.

Amazed by the miracle of this beautiful little child, Abby found her thoughts going to the Bible verse in Jeremiah 1:5: "Before I formed you in the womb I knew you, before you were born I set you apart." Although the child had been left alone on the doorstep, Abby gave thanks that he had never been truly alone. With an unwavering certainty, she knew that God had watched over this precious baby since before he was conceived.

"I wonder what you've been set apart to accomplish," she said to the little one. She bent to kiss his forehead and was met with a faint scent of powder.

In response, he squinched up his face and let loose a squeaky cry that told the women in no uncertain terms that he was ready to be fed.

Ellen had set her tote bag beside the large table in the recreation room and was jotting a note. "We should call Henry so he can take a report," she said, referring to Sergeant Cobb.

Although the Sparrow Island station was only a short distance down Municipal Street, he or any of his deputies could be patrolling anywhere on Sparrow Island or any of the neighboring islands. Ellen had naturally thought to call Henry on his cell phone instead of the local emergency number since the family knew and trusted him. By now the baby had worked up to full throttle in his demand for nourishment.

"I don't think this little guy will be willing to wait for them to show up," Abby said. "Why not call Henry on the way to the Medical Center and ask him to meet us there?"

"Good idea." Ellen locked the door behind them, then followed Abby out to the car. "The baby will need to be checked out by a doctor to make sure there are no health problems."

After Ellen settled into the passenger seat of the small hybrid car, Abby carefully placed the basket in her mother's lap. Ellen gripped it with the tenacity of a bear protecting its cub.

Abby slid into the driver's seat and started the car, her thoughts now shifting from the squalling baby to her mother's sudden shift in demeanor. Just yesterday, she'd been quiet almost to the point of listless, but now her eyes shone bright and she seemed alive with purpose.

After a quick call to Henry, Ellen said a fervent prayer for the child and his parents, whoever they were.

Abby added her own *amen* to her mother's prayer. She knew

that they both felt responsibile for the child's welfare since they were the ones who'd found him. But she thought her mother seemed unusually moved by the child and his situation.

Silently, Abby added a P.S. to the prayer that had just been spoken, asking God to watch over Ellen, as well as the baby.

ABBY WATCHED as Ellen settled onto an examining room chair with the baby and a bottle the nurse had given her. Dr. Randolph had indicated it was pointless to try to examine a hungry baby. Seeing how attached Ellen had become to the little one, the petite blonde doctor had suggested she feed him first and use the opportunity to calm him. Ellen, of course, had quickly agreed.

By now the baby was noisily sucking on the bottle. Ellen smiled down at him, her expression absolutely beatific.

"Henry should be here by the time this little cutie is finished with breakfast. Are you in a hurry?"

Good question. Abby supposed she wanted to get out of here fairly quickly in order to protect her mother from the emotional roller coaster that such an experience was sure to bring. But to come right out and say so would only elicit a protest from Ellen.

"There's no hurry. I guess I'm just anxious," Abby said.

"Me too." Ellen lifted the baby, still wrapped in the beach towel, to her shoulder and gently rubbed his back. "I'm anxious to find out why someone would leave this adorable child to be taken care of by strangers. Something must be terribly wrong in that person's life to do something so drastic."

Dr. Randolph re-entered the room, this time with Sgt. Henry Cobb right behind her. While she listened to the infant's lungs and heart, Henry fired questions at Abby and Ellen.

Just as she had done earlier, Ellen summarized how she'd found the baby. Abby filled in the details of what she'd seen after she arrived. She even offered to make copies of the pictures she'd taken with her digital camera, but he indicated there was no need since he had the actual items in his possession. Henry nodded as she spoke and scribbled some notes in his black spiral-bound book.

Dr. Randolph removed the bonnet and tea-towel diaper and continued the examination. A moment later, Juan Dominguez, the nurse, entered the room with a handful of supplies and took his place beside the doctor at the paper-lined examining table. He quickly popped a pacifier into the child's mouth as the doctor lifted the baby's foot to prick his heel for a blood sample.

To Abby's surprise, the baby flinched but never even whimpered. Instead, Henry winced in sympathy.

Juan grinned at his reaction and prepared to diaper the baby while Dr. Randolph spoke her findings into a handheld tape recorder.

"Healthy, full-term, white male infant. Six pounds, four ounces and twenty inches long. Approximately twelve- to twenty-four hours old."

Healthy. That was the main thing they all wanted to know. Ellen met Abby's gaze and smiled. Abby reached over and squeezed her mother's hand, saying a silent prayer of thanks that the child's physical well-being was off to a good start.

Juan pushed the damp tea towel aside and swiftly fastened a fresh disposable diaper around the baby's bottom.

He looked like a natural despite the fact that he probably didn't have that much experience dealing with newborns. Abby did remember his wife Ana saying that Juan had been very involved in the raising of their three children, who were now grown. Perhaps diaper changing was similar to bicycle riding in that the skill stayed for years after it was needed.

Not that Abby knew much about diaper changing herself. Having never married, she didn't have any children of her own. Sure, she'd practiced occasionally on her niece and nephew, and now on her niece's children. Though it had done the job well enough, her handiwork was sometimes lopsided and barely managed to stay on.

After he slipped a stretch cap and tiny undershirt on the infant and wrapped him in a new receiving blanket, Juan moved to toss the green linen diaper into the trash can.

"I'll need that for evidence." Henry moved forward to intercept the nurse. Though the sheriff was balding, with a fringe of white around his dome, he was nearly six feet tall and had a serious, almost intimidating presence about him.

Juan quickly complied with his request, taking care to drop the item into a plastic bag that read "Biohazard."

"And the hat, the towel and basket," Henry added. "Don't bother, I'll get it."

He nodded toward the box of latex gloves on the counter and asked Dr. Randolph, "Do you mind? We'll need to check for fingerprints, and I don't want to add my own to the broad collection that's already on there."

"Help yourself." Dr. Randolph lifted the child and cradled him gently against her white coat.

As Henry pulled on the gloves and gingerly placed the items in the basket to take with him, Abby sheepishly remembered having pulled the tape loose to peek at the baby. Her fingerprints would be among those added after the baby had been left on the doorstep. Having read her fair share of mystery novels, Abby knew better than to disturb the evidence in a crime scene. But she'd been so surprised by the foundling that her instincts had failed her. Besides, it hadn't actually seemed like a crime scene at the time, but now she supposed there might be a charge for child abandonment or something like that. However, she hoped the focus would be more on helping rather than punishing the person who had done this.

Ellen hovered in front of the doctor, watching affectionately as the baby slipped off to the "land of Nod." "What's going to happen to the baby?" she asked of no one in particular.

His hands still gloved, Henry set the basket on the chair Ellen had just vacated. "He'll stay here at the Medical Center until either a relative comes forward to claim him or we find a foster home for him. Whichever comes first."

"I'll bet it was a teenager who left him there," Ellen suggested. "It would take someone who's very frightened and desperate to leave their baby like that." She addressed her next comment to Dr. Randolph. "I don't know of anyone on the island who was expecting. Do you?"

The doctor handed the baby to Juan with instructions to take him to their rudimentary nursery. Most women in the Islands either delivered their babies at the hospital in Anacortes or had a midwife come to their homes, so the Medical Center didn't often deal with newborns.

After Juan was gone, Dr. Randolph said, "I'm not at liberty to discuss patients' individual medical histories, but I can assure Sergeant Cobb that I'm not aware of anyone who was ready to give birth to a full-term baby."

Abby rubbed a finger along her chin. "Even if it was someone who got their checkups from a doctor on the mainland, on an island this small, it shouldn't be too hard to find out who's expecting. Or rather, who *was* expecting."

Henry raised one eyebrow, the gesture emphasizing the words that followed it. "The officers in District 3 and I will get to the bottom of the matter."

"Don't worry," Dr. Randolph assured Ellen. "We'll take good care of him."

She smiled, but Abby knew that despite the fact that she was grateful to have such a talented, caring doctor looking after the baby, Ellen wasn't thrilled to let him out of her sight.

She and Ellen followed Henry out of the office and into the hallway. As they left, they were greeted with the flash of a camera and a barrage of questions.

CHAPTER ✤ THREE

W HAT'S THIS I HEAR
about you finding a stork egg this morning?" Hugo joked.

Abby's boss, the Curator of the Sparrow Island Nature Conservatory, had changed into long khaki pants and brown hiking shoes to accompany Abby and her group on their short bird-watching excursion this afternoon. Hugo's white hair and white mustache, along with his patrician manner and elegant style of dress, sometimes led people to believe the sixty-five-year-old gentleman wouldn't be interested in anything as outdoorsy as bird-watching. But his intelligence and curiosity, combined with years of traveling the world, had turned him into a sponge. He constantly sought new information and experiences.

The group had ridden together up the winding two-lane road of Mount Ortiz in the conservatory's ten-passenger van. After parking near one of the observation spots, they were now hiking the rest of the way to an outcropping where they'd be able to watch eagles, vultures and other birds swoop and dive from the 1,100-foot cliffs.

Abby admired the fact that, even in casual attire, Hugo still managed to look dapper. Though they would be pushing through underbrush and climbing over fallen trees on their hilly trek, Hugo wore a crisp green polo shirt, a nice leather belt and a new tan cap on which the words *Sparrow Island Nature Conservatory* had been stitched with forest green thread. He looked sharp enough to be photographed for a sportswear catalog. Abby noted that he kept up as well or better than some of the thirty-year-olds on this trip.

Abby had been busy the past few weeks, trying to keep up with the influx of tourists and the extra activities that came with the summer season, which meant that she and Hugo hadn't had much time to spend together lately. But she suspected his sudden interest in joining her group on this afternoon's bird-watching tour was motivated less by his desire to socialize than by his curiosity.

"Word sure travels fast on this island," she said as she picked her way through a tangle of vines that clutched at her ankles.

"William Jansen's hoping the buzz about the baby will cause everyone to rush out and buy a copy of *The Birdcall* when it comes out on Wednesday. I hear he's upping the print run because of this hot scoop."

The fifty-five-year-old editor-in-chief of the island's weekly newspaper loved nothing better than to beat competing papers to print with an exciting news story. And this particular story topped anything that had been printed in *The Birdcall* for quite some time. That was why he'd been so quick to charge to the Medical Center with his camera after he'd heard the dispatch on the police scanner in the paper's office.

Abby pushed her glasses up on her nose. "Well, I hope the

publicity will reunite the baby with his mother and not scare her away."

Jenny Hunsicker, a Little Flock church member who was accompanying her vacationing houseguest on the tour, had overheard their conversation and moved closer to join in.

"Are you talking about the baby that was left at the Senior Center?" Jenny asked. "I wonder if he's going to be put up for adoption."

Abby had heard through the grapevine—namely Janet Heinz, the church secretary who seemed to know about everything that happened in Green Harbor—that Jenny and her husband Steve had been trying for a family for the past couple of years, but so far their prayers hadn't been answered. In her early thirties, Jenny still had time to keep trying, but Abby had seen her grow increasingly disappointed with each unfruitful month that passed.

Jenny's friend Charlotte seemed as eager to hear the answer as she did, leading Abby to wonder if she, too, might be interested in the baby's availability for adoption.

"It's a little too soon for that kind of decision," Abby said, pausing in a clearing near a small outcropping that overlooked the northwestern portion of Sparrow Island and part of the Sound beyond it. "But I heard that he'll be placed in a short-term foster home in a day or so."

Nearby, middle-aged cousins Warren and Conrad playfully jostled each other in an attempt to beat the other to a seat on a rock that presented a breathtaking view of the valley below.

"Hah!" said Warren. "You're getting slow in your old age."

Conrad unfolded the three-legged chair he'd brought with him and flipped to a fresh page in his birding journal. "Doesn't matter. I can still see better than you, Four-Eyes, so I'll just log more bird sightings."

Abby gestured toward a California quail that had taken wing during their somewhat noisy entrance. The men quickly made note of it in their books. Once everyone settled down and got serious about what they'd come here to do, the birds would forget they were here and continue their usual activities.

But Jenny's friend clearly wanted to continue the discussion about the baby.

"I heard about the baby when I was at the craft store at lunch time. The lady who owned the place said she'd sold out of pastel blue yarn because so many people are making blankets and booties for Moses Doe." Charlotte settled down on a blanket beside Jenny and wiped her binocular lenses with a soft cloth.

Abby had instructed the birders to wear dull colors since, unlike four-legged animals, birds could see a broad range of hues. Contrary to her advice, Charlotte sported a scarlet red top. Her excuse had been that it went better with her raven hair than if she'd worn a gray T-shirt.

"Moses Doe?" Abby asked, sitting cross-legged on the ground. The grass stains that spotted a lot of her birding pants were precisely why she didn't spend a lot of money on her wardrobe. "Who called him that?"

"Everybody," said Jenny. "Even the TV anchorman on News at Noon was talking about the baby in the basket. They said the sheriff's department is looking for information about who might have left little Moses."

Abby had fielded a few phone calls today from various friends wanting to know more about the stork's unexpected visit to the Senior Center, but she hadn't realized word of the foundling had already reached the television news station that broadcast out of Seattle. Someone must have called in the news tip.

Eventually, the birders' attention turned back to the birds. While they sat patiently with binoculars to their eyes, Abby quietly described what they were seeing, explaining how the shading beneath the hawks' wings could help them differentiate between the various species.

All in all, this had been a successful day for sighting a variety of both waterfowl and birds of prey. And the birders—especially the two cousins—seemed anxious to head out again tomorrow.

A little later, after Abby and Hugo had returned the vanload of guests to The Bird Nest and were on their way back to the conservatory, Abby broached the subject of her sister's walkathon dilemma. Her boss was an excellent sounding board whenever Abby needed sympathetic ears, and the advice he gave was always wise and carefully thought out.

Although Hugo wasn't on the Skills and Crafts fundraising committee, he sometimes served as a mentor to the children, teaching them about the island's crawling creatures. He hadn't been aware that Mary had been omitted from the walkathon plans. After Abby explained the situation, though, he agreed that the group must have been afraid of creating an uncomfortable situation for Mary.

"She needs to talk to someone on the committee," he said. "Let them know that she wants to help with the planning."

Hugo leaned back in the passenger seat as Abby turned onto Cross Island Road. He toyed with the corner of his mustache.

"She's excellent at organizing," he added. "It would be a shame not to use those talents for the walkathon."

"Unfortunately, it's too late for that. The wheels are already in motion as far as the planning of the walkathon goes."

"Then she should *participate*," Hugo declared and thumped his hand on the door's armrest for emphasis.

"I beg your pardon."

"She wants to help raise money for the Skills and Crafts group, right?" He tugged at the seat belt where it lay across his chest. "So she should gather some sponsors and enter the walkathon just like everybody else. What better way to make her point?"

Abby turned toward Hugo to see if he was serious about what he was suggesting. Although he had a wonderful sense of humor when the situation called for it, she knew he wouldn't make a joke out of something like this.

The tires bumped along the right edge of the road, and Abby straightened the wheel to compensate for the drift.

"You're serious, aren't you?"

"Couldn't be more serious if my hair was on fire. Tell her to sign me up as her first sponsor."

Abby smiled, imagining her sister's response to the friendly challenge. Abby knew that Mary wouldn't want to risk looking like a whiner—or worse, hurting her friends' feelings when she knew they only meant well—by complaining to the committee or taking the matter to Rev. Hale. But this solution allowed Mary to do what she did best—take action.

"Hugo Baron," Abby said, "Has anyone ever told you that you're a genius?"

AFTER SHE RETURNED THE VAN to the conservatory, Abby drove her car the short distance down Primrose Lane to Stanton Farm. She would pop in for a moment to check on her mother

before heading home to the tetrazzini dinner Mary had promised. And, of course, she'd see if Ellen had heard any more news
about the baby.

Abby passed the pick-your-own lavender patch near the
front of the twenty-five-acre farm and was surprised to find the
driveway filled with cars. Mary's van was parked conveniently
close to the ramp that led to the front door, and nearby were
cars she quickly identified as belonging to Bobby's parents,
Emma Stoltz, the Flemmings from next door, and others that
she couldn't immediately place. Perhaps these people had come
to hear Ellen's firsthand account of finding the baby at the
Senior Center.

After a quick knock, acknowledged by a single *woof!* from
Finnegan, Abby opened the door to a roomful of people speaking in hushed tones. In addition to the folks she'd identified by
their cars outside, Janet Heinz and Terza Choi were there. Even
Sam the farmhand had stayed past his usual work time.

The visitors clustered in the living room shot quick glances
in her direction and murmured greetings, then turned their
attention back to Ellen who sat in her favorite chair beside
George.

But the real focus of their attention was the blanketed bundle in Ellen's arms. An empty bottle sat on the end table beside
her chair.

"Mom?"

Ellen looked up and fixed Abby with eyes that stirred her to
the core. In her mother's expression was a blend of love, determination, pain, compassion and strength. It was a look not
unlike the one she'd worn during Mary's recovery from her
accident.

"I couldn't stand to let him spend his first days in a clinic," Ellen said. "The nurses there are wonderful, but a medical center is not a home."

An uneasy feeling settled in the pit of Abby's stomach. She took a seat on the couch beside Sam.

"His placement here is only temporary, of course," Ellen continued. "I'll only have him for up to two weeks, hopefully less if we can reunite him with his family sooner."

Joanne opened a magazine on the coffee table and motioned for Beau to look at the picture. "I'm glad Ellen kept up her certification to be an emergency foster parent," she piped in. "I have my hands full with Beau, and the others were either out of town or not available to take him right now."

"Are you sure this is a good idea?" Abby asked, her tone soft. "Taking care of a newborn is tiring even for people in their twenties."

George smiled and touched his wife's arm. "I'll be here to help out. We'll manage just fine."

"That's right," said Ellen. "We've done it before, we can do it again."

Bobby had been making the rounds in the room, passing a sheet of paper around, which each family signed. Then he brought it to Abby. The childish handwriting at the top read, "Skills and Crafts—Walkathon Pledges."

Abby added her signature to the list and filled in an amount that was less than what she'd budgeted for the charity. The remainder would go on Mary's sponsor sheet, provided her sister agreed to participate in the event.

"I thought the sponsor sheets and instructions were going to be distributed at church on Wednesday night," she said.

"They are," Bobby confirmed. "I'm just getting a head start."

She certainly admired his enthusiasm. But then Abby remembered what Mary had said about the boy's competitive attitude toward the event. Perhaps his "head start" was more about winning prizes than about raising money for a good cause.

Beau toddled away from the coffee table, but Bobby blocked him from leaving the room. The child had tired of looking at pictures and started to wander off to search for other entertainment. Hooking a finger through his overall strap, Bobby gently steered the child back to the Flemmings.

"It's a good thing you kept the crib and all that baby stuff from Mary's grandkids," Bobby said as he folded the paper and stuffed it in his pants pocket. "Otherwise Moses would have to sleep in a dresser drawer."

Abby looked at Ellen and recalled her mother's comparison of the child's discovery to the early prophet. "Is his name really Moses?"

Ellen smiled down at the child. "Henry thought it made sense to refer to him as Moses Doe, seeing as how the baby was found in a basket."

Clint Flemming laughed at the image Bobby had presented of the baby sleeping in the furniture. He ruffled his foster son's hair. "Yeah, they're a lot easier to take care of when they stay in one place."

Abby knew the neighbor's comment wasn't a complaint. At fifty-seven, a few years younger than his wife, Clint willingly shared the responsibilities of caring for the rambunctious child who'd been living with them for the past several months.

Abby knew that her father—and lots of others in Green Harbor—would happily extend all the help Ellen needed to care for the little one. What she didn't know was whether the emotional upheaval of attaching to the child and then having him taken away would be too much for her mother to handle.

Ellen lifted the sleeping child to her shoulder and snuggled him. "I didn't do this on a whim," she told Abby, but it seemed as though she was addressing everyone else as well. "I prayed about it, talked to George and we prayed some more. God laid it on our hearts to help this child. If our hearts hurt when the baby leaves, then God will help us through it."

Abby smiled. Their heavenly father would take care of the baby, even though his earthly parents had let him down. And He would take care of the rest of them, too.

"I should have known you wouldn't have been impulsive in your decision," she acknowledged with a laugh. "Not after all the times you told Mary and me, 'think and pray before you act!'"

"I'll put your family and the baby on the prayer list at church," Janet promised. The secretary loved to stay in touch with what was going on in the community and she often brought concerns back to the church for prayer. Some people called what she did gossiping, but Abby knew that Janet's eagerness to know about everyone's comings and goings was driven by a loving concern. And, of course, a heaping dose of curiosity.

"Don't forget Henry and his deputies," Mary reminded her friend. "They'll need God's help in locating the person who left Moses there for others to find."

Abby rubbed a finger along her jaw. "No leads yet?"

If anyone in the room would know, it would be Mary, given that she was dating the deputy sheriff. But Abby's older sister shook her head. "Not yet, but they're good at what they do. It won't be long."

Sandy McDonald scooted over on the upholstered chair to make room for Bobby to squeeze in beside her. She concurred with Mary, but added her own theory. "It's probably a teenage mother who was scared and desperate. They're so impulsive at that age."

And she should know. The thirty-one-year-old English teacher taught all grade levels at Green Harbor School. The stories she brought home ranged from funny to sad to downright infuriating at times. But no matter the situation, the common factor was her kindhearted persistence through it all.

"Were there any expectant teens at school?" George asked.

Janet answered for her. "If there had been, everybody would have known about it. You can't keep many secrets on an island this small."

Bobby bounced beside his mother. "Maybe Moses was left by a tourist."

All eyes turned to Neil McDonald, who was still wearing the light blue work shirt that made his tanned face and arms seem even darker than they already were. His job on the ferry brought him into contact with hundreds of passengers a day, tourists and locals alike.

He frowned and closed his cinnamon brown eyes as he considered the possibility. "I don't know," he said, opening his eyes at last. "I see all kinds of people. If a lady is obviously expecting, I try to make sure she's seated where there's not so much rocking motion. But some people just sit in their cars during the crossing. It's possible someone came over and I didn't even see them."

Clint Flemming accepted the squirming child that Joanne placed in his lap. "It wouldn't make sense for someone from the mainland to come to a small community where they'd be more likely to be noticed." He grabbed the wriggling Beau in a bear hug, then bounced the boy on his knee. "Seems to me it would be the other way around, with the mother going to a big city where she could be anonymous."

Sam had been standing silently near the door, taking it all in. Now he offered his own theory. "Who's to say that it was the mother who left Moses in the basket? For all we know, the baby could have been kidnapped. Then maybe the kidnapper panicked and they left him at the Senior Center to be found and returned to the mother."

Abby understood why Sam's thoughts took this turn. Having spent time in prison before coming to work for the Stantons, he'd seen the seamier side of life. He knew the ease with which hardened criminals perpetrated their crimes, never once thinking about the victims of their actions, but only about what they themselves could gain.

"Henry's sent a notice to all the hospitals in Washington," Mary said, "to see if perhaps one of their babies is missing."

Now Janet's mother, Emma Stoltz, picked up the thread. "If that were the case, wouldn't we have heard about it on the news?"

"No, this baby wasn't born in a hospital," Abby declared.

Ellen straightened from kissing the infant's fuzz-covered head. "How do you know that?" she asked. "Because he wasn't wearing hospital clothes or a real diaper?"

"That's part of it." Abby thought back to this morning when she'd inspected under the towel that covered the baby. "When a child is born at a hospital, they clamp off the umbilical cord with a plastic clip. At least that's what I saw on my friends' babies and grandchildren."

"Yes," said Ellen. "That's what's on Moses now."

"But it wasn't there this morning. What I saw was a narrow

blue ribbon . . . the kind you'd buy at a sewing notions store. In fact, it looked just like the ribbon in his handkerchief bonnet." Abby took a slow, deep breath as she tried to tie the pieces of this puzzle together. "Dr. Randolph must have replaced the ribbon with a sterile clamp to reduce the risk of infection."

Clint rose and stretched, and Beau mimicked his actions. "When you folks solve this mystery, let us know, will you? We've got to duck out so this little guy can get some shut-eye."

The McDonalds followed them out, citing a workday tomorrow as their reason for leaving. The others took this as their cue, and after all the good-byes were said, only Terza stayed behind with the Stantons.

The Chinese woman busied herself with moving knick-knacks from the end tables and placing them on the mantel.

Ellen handed the baby to George, then rose from her chair. "Don't worry about that, Terza. Moses isn't going to be here long enough to get into any mischief."

"Doesn't matter," Terza insisted. "The baby needs us to keep him safe."

George just grinned in amusement, then excused himself to change the diaper and put Moses to bed.

"It's amazing how quickly it's all coming back for us," Ellen said, referring to their child care skills. "Of course, it helped that we've had refresher courses with Emily and Nicholas."

Mary's seven- and three-year-old grandchildren lived in Florida with Mary's daughter and her husband. Whenever the family came to Sparrow Island for a visit, Ellen and George spent as much time with them as possible, partly for themselves and partly to give the children's parents a break.

Finnegan sat up, his yellow ears cocked forward as he watched Terza move busily through the room. She picked up a pillow from the sofa and examined the fabric-covered button. "That's on tight. I don't think it will be a problem for the baby."

Her actions were so purposeful that no one felt inclined to question them. The Stantons—and Finnegan—formed a semicircle around Terza as they watched her hyper movements, but she was so intent on what she was doing that she seemed not to notice them at all.

She dropped the pillow back on the couch, then flitted over to the decorative bookcase where Ellen had arranged a number of photos and the ceramic pieces the grandchildren and great-grandchildren had made in school. By now, George had returned from diapering and putting the baby to bed.

Terza pressed gently against the bookshelf, and it rocked slightly under her hands. "That needs to be stabilized," she informed George. "I'll ask Martin to come over tomorrow and help."

George cleared his throat. "That's not really necessar—"

But Terza was on a mission. Now she leaned over the back of the sofa to tie the drapery cords so short that even she had a hard time reaching them. "There," she declared. "Nobody will choke on these. Can't ever be too safe."

As she drew her hand away, her finger dragged along the venetian blind slat. She drew in a quick breath and squeezed the finger with her thumb.

A tiny pool of blood stained her finger.

"Oh, Terza, you're hurt!" Ellen rushed toward her and ushered her to the kitchen where she helped her wash the wound, and George went to the utility closet to retrieve a bandage.

Mary turned her chair toward Abby. "You have any idea what that was all about?"

"Not a clue."

CHAPTER 🌸 FOUR

THE TUESDAY LUNCH CROWD
had hit the Springhouse Café hard today. It was almost as busy
as last week when the Fourth-of-July vacationers had swarmed
the island.

Mary waved from a table by the window as Abby brought
in her group of nine for lunch. Hugo had stayed at the conservatory this morning, working on the museum's next fundraising project.

Seated with Mary was Henry, obviously on duty since he
was wearing his green sergeant's uniform. Abby motioned that
she'd be back momentarily, then led Charlotte to the ladies'
room while the rest of the birders scattered themselves among
the open tables. While the young woman washed at the sink,
Abby retrieved an antibacterial salve from one of the pockets
on her vest.

Charlotte held out her arm, inner side up, while Abby
applied medicine to the scrape that ran from wrist to elbow.

"That's gotta hurt," Abby said when the dark-haired woman
sucked air between her teeth.

"Not as much as finding out what a backstabber my friend is," Charlotte said. "Sorry about messing up your schedule."

The plan had been to break for a picnic lunch, then move on to the observation tower where they'd watch the alder-shaded water's edge for signs of wood ducks, cinnamon teals, hawks, kingfishers and gadwalls. However, from the time everyone had piled into the van this morning, the air had been filled, not with birdcalls, but with minor squabbles and disagreements.

It seemed to Abby that it was easier to blend into the environment when a group's demeanor was relaxed and cheerful rather than prickling with tension. The college chums, Charlotte and Jenny, had been anything but chummy. Abby noticed that most of their disagreements had been provoked or worsened by Charlotte's negative attitude. In addition, cousins Warren and Conrad had been teasingly swiping each other's birding journals, jostling each other, and in general acting like a couple of boisterous preteens. The other birders, a married couple and two elderly sisters, had started out in a good mood but eventually absorbed the tension from the others and ended up retreating into an uneasy silence.

Abby had to hand it to the four of them for trying to get the group back on track. Elaine, a cheerful woman who looked to be in her early seventies but proudly declared her herself to be eighty-four, had tried to interest the others in stories about the horses she raised and still rode every day. When that didn't work, her younger sister Delphine had launched into extolling the merits of camouflaging gray hair with blonde highlights.

Even the married couple had felt compelled to advise the feuding friends and competing cousins about the importance of compromise and tolerance. Shelley and Tom were less than a year away from celebrating their thirtieth anniversary and had weathered their share of marital storms over the years. Shelley shared that by changing her own responses to the occasional bothersome things that Tom did, it had changed the entire dynamic of the relationship.

Unfortunately, Conrad and Warren were bent on continuing their sophomoric behavior, and Jenny and Charlotte were too focused on their own hurt feelings to listen to what the others had to say.

"I suppose everybody could use a break," Abby said noncommittally. "Maybe we'll all feel better after a nice lunch and cooling off in the air conditioning."

"It'll take more than air conditioning to cool me off," Charlotte said. She blew on her arm to dry the salve. "I wouldn't have tripped over that root if Jenny hadn't distracted me by talking about the baby. She knew I was thinking about adopting Moses, but then she jumped on the bandwagon and started talking about adopting him herself. What kind of friend would do something like that?"

Abby opened the door and followed Charlotte out of the ladies' room. "You know, there's still a good chance that the authorities will find his mother. Besides, there are plenty of other children who are waiting to be welcomed into good homes."

Charlotte muttered something under her breath.

As the pair returned to the front of the restaurant, they walked past Warren and Conrad's table where the cousins knocked a fork to the floor as each sought to dominate the other in a game of arm wrestling.

At the table by the window that looked out over Randolph Bay, Jenny stood with her hands on her knees, engaged in a conversation with Henry, who furrowed his eyebrows at what she was saying.

As Abby and Charlotte approached them, they overheard Jenny talking about the foundling and her interest in becoming his mother.

Charlotte's eyes widened. She marched over to her friend and grabbed her by the elbow. "What do you think you're doing?" she demanded. "I already told you I was going to apply to adopt Moses. It's always about what you want, isn't it? First it was the valedictorian position in high school, then the guy I liked in college. And now this!"

Charlotte swept both arms outward as if to indicate that her friend wanted the entire world.

Jenny had spent most of the morning trying to smooth Charlotte's ruffled feathers. But now it appeared as though she had reached her limit. Even so, her voice grew soft, as if she was more hurt than angry.

"Why are you doing this to me, Char? I want Moses because I haven't been able to conceive a baby of my own. Unlike some people I know," she said pointedly, "I'm not considering adoption just to preserve my waistline."

Charlotte drew herself up in a huff. "Is this how you treat all your houseguests?" She turned her attention to Henry. "Sergeant Cobb, what do I have to do to be selected as the baby's adoptive parent?"

Henry stood and cleared his throat. A heavy flashlight and baton dangled from his black utility belt. "Ladies, it's not my decision to make."

His authoritative presence seemed to have a calming influence over Jenny, but Charlotte grew even more determined to hold her ground.

"This is no way for friends to act toward each other," he said. "You should be supporting each other at a time like this."

"He's right," Jenny said and nodded toward a nearby table that a family had just vacated. "Let's go sit over there and get this resolved. I don't want us bitter toward each other."

Charlotte put a hand on her tiny waist and lifted her chin. "No, thank you. I'm going to go wait outside. By myself."

As she stalked over to the exit, Jenny's entire demeanor seemed to crumple. She paused for a moment, as if deciding what to do next. Then she tightened her lip and excused herself to join Elaine and Delphine at their table. The sisters immediately welcomed her with expressions of sympathy for her friendship troubles and recommendations as to what looked good on the menu.

Mary motioned to Abby. "Sit down," Mary said, patting the chair beside her. "Ida will be back in a minute to bring us some coffee. Even if Henry has to rush off, I can wait with you while you eat."

Not wanting to intrude on their time together, Abby paused, but Henry insisted that she join them.

Smiling her thanks, Abby slid onto the worn wooden chair. She silently thanked God for bringing this wonderful man into her sister's life. Henry was selfless, both in his job and in his relationships, and he never missed an opportunity to do a good deed. For that, Abby was grateful, because she could use a little of their positive energy after the morning she'd had.

"I don't know what's gotten into everyone," she said. "It's like people have forgotten the golden rule and are entirely focused on getting what they want for themselves."

Mary reached over and patted her hand as Ida swooped to the table and poured coffee into their cups.

"Hi, Abby." The blonde ponytailed waitress turned to Henry and Mary. "Sorry it took me so long to get back over here. A new girl started working this week and she's been poaching my tables. I needed to set that straight before it becomes a habit."

Abby glanced at her sister with an expression that said, "See what I mean?"

Most of Ida's income came from tips, so this was no small affront. However, Abby was pleased that her young friend had been both assertive and kind in handling the matter. When Abby had first met the twenty-four-year-old, Ida had been very shy and sometimes tongue-tied. But since attending Little Flock, where the members had embraced her into the church family, she had made great improvements in coming out of her shell.

Abby returned the menu to Ida without even looking at it and ordered today's special: shrimp salad on a bed of lettuce and shredded carrots.

Before it arrived, however, the radio on Henry's hip squawked and announced an address on Orcas Island. Although one of the deputies reported that he was on the way, Henry excused himself. He gave Mary a quick kiss and promised to call her.

As he was headed out the door, Mary paused and said a brief prayer, asking God to watch over Henry and the people he helped.

Abby bowed her head, too, recalling that when she'd lived in New York, she had occasionally passed traffic accidents to which police, fire or rescue personnel had already arrived. At those times, she'd always said a prayer for the people involved in the fender benders, as well as for the people attending to their needs. Later, Mary's accident had involved a deer, rain-slicked roads and a deep ravine. Henry, thank God, had been the one to find Mary's wrecked car. Now that Abby had come to know and care about Henry, that put a personal face on all the saints of the road she'd prayed for over the years.

The sisters sat in companionable silence for a while, Mary sipping her coffee and Abby savoring the colorful meal that tantalized her taste buds.

Eventually, Abby couldn't stand it any longer. She'd hoped Mary would give her an opener to the subject she wanted to discuss, but Mary seemed preoccupied with whatever was churning in her mind.

"Have you talked to the walkathon committee?" Abby asked.

Mary looked up and blinked as if surprised that Abby had spoken what had been tumbling through her thoughts. "As a result of the walkathon, there will be seed money to buy the supplies needed to start a new Skills and Crafts group in Seattle. How can I object to that?" She set her coffee cup down and ran her finger around the rim. "No, I'm just going to let it slide. The important thing is that God's work is getting done."

Abby loved her sister's wise and generous heart. But despite Mary's easy response, Abby knew that she was not completely satisfied with the situation.

"When you and Candace receive a shipment of flowers at Island Blooms," Abby said, referring to the shop Mary owned, and the woman who managed it, "and some of the flowers are perfect, but a few are already starting to dry up, do you throw the bad ones away?"

At the abrupt change of topic, Mary gave her a hesitant sidelong glance. "You know we don't throw anything away. The flowers that can't be revived are plucked of their petals and sold as potpourri. What's leftover is saved to be used as compost in Dad's garden."

"So you use all of the flowers . . . even the bad parts?"

"Of course." Mary narrowed her eyes. "What are you getting at?"

Abby smiled and leaned her forearms against the table's edge. "Just that God uses the bad parts of our experiences, too. Helping to form the new Skills and Crafts group is a beautiful thing, and it serves a wonderful purpose. But, like the wilted rose petals, the walkathon committee's failure to include you in the planning is also an opportunity to turn an ugly flower into sweet-smelling potpourri."

Mary picked up her spoon and stirred the milky brown liquid at the bottom of her cup. "If I don't take those wilted roses from the wrapping and air them out, they can turn soggy and grow mold."

"You don't want your relationship with the other leaders in the Skills and Crafts group to turn soggy and grow mold." Abby was pleased that Mary understood what she'd been trying to say and even took the analogy a step further. "I have an idea how you can take your roses out of the wrapping."

Then Abby relayed the conversation she'd had with Hugo and his suggestion that Mary enter the walkathon herself.

"Some of the walkathon route is on the sidewalks around Green Harbor," Mary said, "but most of it follows bicycle trails."

"I'm not saying it will be easy," Abby conceded. "But nothing worth having is easy."

Mary laughed, causing Finnegan to rise from his position under the table to see what was so funny. "I can see it now," she said, holding her hands together like a picture frame. "The kids reach the finish line early in the afternoon. Later that night, as the moon is coming up, Finnegan will be at home in his doggy bed while I'm still pushing along on the trail with blisters the size of cantaloupes on my hands."

Okay, so maybe she was poking fun at herself, but her laughter was a vast improvement over the troubled thoughtfulness that had dominated their meal earlier. This moment of mirth reminded Abby why she was so glad to be this incredible woman's sister.

"Sure, you probably won't be breaking the finish-line tape," Abby admitted, "but would you be entering to win or entering to make a difference?"

At that, Mary's laughter faded away and her expression grew serious. "I want to make a difference," she said. "First, for the children on the mainland who need this new Skills and Crafts group. And I want to show people that just because I can't walk, that doesn't mean I can't make a difference."

The grit and determination had filtered back into her voice, for which Abby was grateful. "So you'll do it?"

Mary shrugged. "I obviously wouldn't be entering to win."

"So the last will be first and the first will be last," Abby said, quoting Matthew 20:16.

"I haven't said I'd do it," Mary reminded her. "This is something that needs prayer."

"Of course," Abby agreed. She wouldn't push. After all, it had been merely a suggestion. She felt confident that Mary would do whatever God led her to do.

THE FELLOWSHIP HALL in Little Flock bustled with activity on Wednesday night. Fortunately, handyman Rick DeBow had made it his first priority to set up a dehumidifier to be used in the church whenever the weather turned as warm as it had last week. Now the contraption hummed along efficiently, removing some of the humidity from the rooms to make it a more comfortable learning environment.

Abby had come for the adult Bible study, which was not set to start for another twenty minutes, and Mary was here to help with the children's Skills and Crafts group.

They paused outside Janet Heinz's office for Abby to collect the new study guides, but the door was closed. She lifted her hand to knock, but the secretary flitted past and waved a handful of booklets at her.

"Don't go in there. Rev. Hale's finishing up a counseling session. Is this what you need?" Janet handed Abby the new Bible study guides.

"Yes, thank you." Abby took the booklets and glanced through them while Janet dashed off to handle some other administrative need.

The scripture for tonight's lesson was 2 Timothy 2:5: "Similarly, if anyone competes as an athlete, he does not receive the victor's crown unless he competes according to the rules."

It seemed to be an apt choice, especially considering the upcoming walkathon. However, Abby's mind wasn't on tonight's lesson, but on the outcome of Mary's prayers.

She wanted to ask her sister if she'd decided to enter the walkathon. Although she was curious, she considered it best to give Mary her space and not make her feel pressured.

Bobby broke away from the group of children clustered at the far end of the fellowship hall and came to join Abby and Mary. His short brown hair pointed in every direction but down, and the freckles across his nose had darkened under the summer sun.

"Guess what, Mary?" He shook a paper with a long list of

names on it in front of her. Then he danced around her chair while Finnegan watched with curious patience. "I've got a whole bunch of people signed up already. I think I'm going to win the prize for having the most sponsors."

"Good for you," she said and reached out to grab him for a quick hug. "If you win, let me know and I'll take you on in a game."

The prize—a folding, tabletop Ping-Pong set—had spurred a fierce but friendly competition among the members of the Skills and Crafts group. There would be other prizes, as well, and the children were charged up to do their best to win them.

Abby peered over at the rambling list of names on the paper Bobby clutched in his hand. "The walkathon was only announced Sunday. How did you manage to sign up so many sponsors already?"

One of her duties as Associate Curator was to raise funds for the conservatory. Her young friend was obviously a natural salesman. If he had any fresh ideas for motivating people to help, then she'd love to hear them.

Bobby shifted his attention back to the group of children that was starting to migrate to their classroom. "*Um*, they're getting ready to start the meeting."

"I'm right behind you," Mary said and pushed off to join the group.

Abby tucked the study guides to her chest and was preparing to go to the sanctuary where her Bible group was gathering, but before she'd crossed the foyer, the main door opened and in came Ellen and Terza.

Between them, each woman gripped the handle of a blanket-covered car-to-carrier device. Their unexpected arrival incited a cluster of onlookers to *ooh* and *ahh* over the child. Even

Thelma Rogers, who could always find the dark lining in any cloud, beamed down at the baby as she tweaked his bootied toe.

Janet's office door opened behind Abby. She turned to see Tamara Preston, the young woman her mother knew from working at the Senior Center, and a handsome blond man emerge with Rev. Hale.

The pastor seemed thoughtful, the way he looked when he was trying to make an important point in one of his sermons. The young man, presumably Tamara's husband, was as tall and slim as she was short and heavy, and his golden tan contrasted sharply with her pale, almost gray complexion.

Tamara sidled close and gazed up at him with adoring blue eyes. Abby was somewhat disturbed to notice that he seemed unaware of her show of affection.

He reached past her to shake Rev. Hale's hand, then turned to leave. He was maneuvering past the women huddled around Ellen and Terza when Tamara paused to peer past them to catch a glimpse of the baby.

Her husband had already opened the door to leave when he noticed Tamara wasn't with him. Letting the door close again, he stood with his hand on the doorknob and sighed.

However, Tamara was oblivious to his impatience. She stood on the outskirts of the group until Terza noticed and motioned her closer.

"Let Tamara see," the tiny woman commanded, and the others parted like the Red Sea.

But even though they'd made room for her, she only inched a little closer. Abby smiled as she wondered whether the young woman was afraid the little one might spit up or create some other kind of mess. Not having children herself, Abby understood her cautious approach.

"Do you want to hold him?" Ellen asked as one of the ladies handed the carrier back to her.

The young woman looked torn between accepting Ellen's invitation and hurrying to keep her husband from waiting any longer.

Abby joined the tiny throng and was about to say something when Tamara's husband called from his post by the door.

"Tamara, I thought you said you weren't feeling well." His brown eyes darkened, and it was obvious that he was used to being in a hurry.

Abby recalled Tamara saying that her husband traveled a lot for his job and was busily climbing the corporate ladder.

Tamara gave Ellen a half smile. "Maybe later," she said hopefully.

As the cluster broke up, Abby handed the booklets to Thelma and asked her to take them to the Bible study group.

Terza remained with Ellen and the baby. It was as if she had declared herself the child's honorary aunt. Abby was glad for her interest in little Moses, for Terza had been a big help to Ellen for the past couple of days. Fortunately, her big-hearted husband had been willing to pick up her duties at The Bird Nest so she could spend time with Ellen.

Ellen shifted her weight from foot to foot, rocking the baby as she did so.

Abby smiled at her mother. "Did you come to show Moses off and satisfy everyone's curiosity?"

Terza shifted her gaze to Ellen, then touched her arm. The small gesture softened the anxious expression that crossed Ellen's face.

Ellen cleared her throat. "That was part of it. Mostly, I needed to talk to you."

A frown of concern pulled Abby's eyebrows together. "What's wrong? Is Moses okay?"

The moment she asked the question, she knew that Moses was fine. Her mother wouldn't have taken him out of the house if he'd shown any signs of being sick.

It was something else that had prompted Ellen to come here tonight and seek her out. Something rather troubling, given her air of distress.

"He's fine. Eating like a piglet, in fact."

Terza grinned at the comparison, then immediately donned an expression of concern.

"I had a visit from the social worker this afternoon." Ellen shifted the baby to her other arm.

Abby stepped forward to take the heavy bundle from her mother. As she put the sleepy child to her shoulder, he immediately drew his knees up under his body. Abby rested her cheek against the child's dark fuzz-covered head and enjoyed the sweet smell of baby powder. She held her free hand securely against his rounded back and was amazed once again how God had designed everything, even people, to fit together just so.

"She said a long-term family has been found for Moses," Ellen continued.

When Abby spoke her voice was soft, partly to avoid jarring Moses from his snoozing and partly to soothe her mother.

"You were expecting this," she said. "You said yourself that you wanted him to be able to settle in with a family and not be moved from pillar to post."

"I wanted him to be able to settle in with *his* family."

Although the note that had been left in the baby's basket had indicated that his mother was unable to provide a proper family for him, it was everyone's hope that whatever troubles had led her to take such drastic measures could be resolved with the support of the community.

This morning, when Abby had led the birding group to a heavily wooded area at the northeastern corner of the island, they'd come across a spotted fawn that had been separated from its mother. Confused and frightened, the young deer had wandered aimlessly back and forth, its huge ears swiveling to detect a sound that would indicate its mother's return.

Eventually, it folded its spindly legs and sank to the ground where it settled in a curled-up ball to wait.

The birders had seemed more fearful than the fawn and they were convinced that harm would come to the young animal. But after a while the mother was observed a short distance away, watching and waiting until the time was right. When the doe finally rejoined her fawn, it was all the bird-watchers could do to keep from cheering.

Abby wanted the same for Moses and his mother. But she knew that regardless of where she might be, their heavenly father was watching over both.

"Me, too, Mom. But we should be thankful that there's someone who's willing to love him until his birth family is located." The baby squirmed in her arms and Abby patted him until he settled down. "Perhaps you can visit him while Henry continues the search for the mother."

"That's the problem," Terza interjected. "The new foster family lives on the mainland."

To Abby's astonishment, her mother teared up and brushed away the moisture with the heel of her hand.

Still resting her wrist against the child's back, Abby pushed her glasses up with her finger and spoke gently. "I don't see how this is a problem. You've been saying all along that you want what's best for Moses. So as long as he's placed with a good family, that's a good thing. Right?"

Still red-eyed, Ellen seemed to grope for words. She looked at Terza as if hoping she could help. "I'm afraid that if he leaves Sparrow Island, it'll be . . . it'll be as if . . ."

She sniffed and rubbed her eyes, unable to finish.

Terza touched her arm and rubbed it gently. Then, so softly that Abby could barely hear, she said, "As if he never existed."

CHAPTER ✤ FIVE

So ARE YOU SAYING MOM doesn't want to turn Moses over to the new foster parents?" Mary asked later that evening after Abby relayed the discussion she'd had with Ellen and Terza.

"No, that's not it at all." Abby brought two cups of herbal tea into the living room and set one down next to Mary then took a seat on the sofa. She enjoyed it when they had tea and conversation to unwind before bed. Tonight was no exception. Talking with Mary always helped her clear her mind and straighten her perspective on matters. She just hoped that Mary would be able to help her understand their mother's distress over this matter concerning Moses. "Mom was upset about the plans to send him off the island. She seems to think that he'll be forgotten once he's gone."

"What did Terza think of that?"

Abby blew across the top of her tea before she took a sip. Blossom, Mary's white Persian cat, crossed the sofa and stepped on Abby's lap to sniff the steam that rose from her cup.

Abby moved the cup away from the cat to prevent a burn, but Blossom scrunched her face into a half sneer as if to indicate she wouldn't have been interested unless it had been catnip tea.

"That's the weird part. Terza seemed to understand exactly what Mom was saying about Moses disappearing off everybody's radar screen once he's off the island and out of the limelight."

Mary didn't respond, but just sat and sipped her tea. Finally, after a moment, she said, "At least she's not acting withdrawn like she'd been before she found Moses."

"Yeah, that was weird," Abby agreed. "I wish Dad would tell us why she goes through those strange moods every summer."

"Do you think he knows?"

Abby stretched back on the couch and Blossom rolled onto her back for a belly rub, which Abby obliged. "He probably has at least a guess as to why Mom gets so quiet the first half of every July."

"I used to think it had something to do with the Fourth of July tourists. But she was like that long before she ever started working part-time for the Visitors Center." Mary picked up *The Birdcall*, and held it up, front page out, for Abby to see. "This is a good picture of you and Mom coming out of the Medical Center. Were you wearing blush?"

Abby almost laughed as her sister's focus turned to beauty matters. Mary was deep and caring, and possessed all the wonderful traits that mattered most in a person, but she also loved beautifying everything around her. Sometimes that involved experimenting with makeup or bold-colored blouses such as the royal blue and silver top she wore now. Other times it involved a bright new bedspread or maybe a bit of fresh paint to liven things up. Mostly, she put her beautifying efforts to work at Island Blooms, creating unique and colorful floral arrangements to cheer up her customers.

"No, that was pure adrenaline," Abby said, recalling the surprise and excitement that accompanied finding little Moses just two days ago.

Finnegan rose from the spot where he'd been resting on the other side of the room and gave a little woof accompanied by a friendly tail wag. Mary had already taken off his service cape, a cue that he was off duty for the rest of the night, but the dog liked to stay close where he could keep watch over his mistress.

A moment later a light tap sounded at the front door.

"I'll get it," Abby said as much to Finnegan as to Mary. The door handle was rigged so that, if necessary, the dog could pull a leather strap to open it. Abby set her cup in the middle of the coffee table where Blossom wasn't likely to bother it and went to let their visitor in.

She suspected even before she opened the door that it was Henry. He had been putting in extra hours the past couple of days, working to uncover the identity of the person who'd left baby Moses at the Senior Center, so he was probably stopping by to tell Mary goodnight before heading home to Lopez Island for the evening.

After venturing a quick peek through the small window, Abby opened the door and said to her sister, "Hey, Mary, there's a handsome man in a uniform standing on our porch. Want me to let him in?"

Even at the end of a long day, Henry looked sharp in his desert tan shirt with dark green tie and pants. The seven-pointed gold star on the left side of his shirt gleamed with authority. Abby imagined that the sight of this man responding to an emergency call must fill citizens with a sense of comfort and security.

Mary turned toward her boyfriend who practically filled the doorway with the breadth of his shoulders. A girlish smile spread across her face. "Why would an officer be coming to my house? I haven't committed any crimes."

Henry nodded a greeting to Abby, then politely stepped past her to give his full attention to Mary. "Ah, but I have evidence that you stole the radiance from the sunshine and put it in your eyes," he said with a playful wink. "Then you kidnapped my heart and locked it behind your smile. That's a felony offense."

"Maybe I should call a locksmith to set you free?"

He bent and gave her a little kiss. "Don't you dare."

"How about some chamomile tea?" Abby asked after he'd taken the seat on the sofa that she'd just vacated.

"Thank you," he said and gave an ecstatic Finnegan some friendly rubs while Blossom nuzzled under his arm and left white hairs on his pants. "That would be nice."

What was nice was that her sister had such a warm and compassionate man to keep her company. Abby dawdled in the kitchen to give the couple time to greet each other privately.

When she returned a few minutes later, their conversation had turned from personal matters to what seemed to be the only topic of interest on Sparrow Island this week . . . Moses.

Henry pushed a hand through the fringe of white hair that skirted the sides and back of his head. "No fingerprints anywhere."

Abby handed Henry his tea and took a seat in the over-stuffed chair beside Mary. "Not even on the duct tape or The Green Grocer sack covering the baby's diaper?"

"Just a fragment, but not enough to enter into the computer database. And even that was smudged."

At Mary's disappointed expression, he added, "Most likely, the person who left Moses is not someone with a criminal record anyway. It was probably someone in their teens or early twenties who felt desperate but didn't know where to turn for help."

That was exactly what Abby had surmised the other morning with her mother, but something didn't seem quite right about that explanation. "So you're saying it was someone who was clever enough to wipe off fingerprints before leaving Moses for Mom to find."

Mary wouldn't give up on the possibility that technology might provide the answer. "There's always DNA. Dr. Randolph took blood samples from the baby. Now all you have to do is match it to the parents." She seemed extraordinarily pleased with herself for having thought of this. "According to the crime shows I've seen on TV, you can even match the baby's DNA to family members other than the parents."

"First of all, Hollywood takes a lot of liberties with the facts surrounding forensics," Henry said. Even though he disagreed with Mary's suggestion, his tone did not seem to be scornful of the fact that, like so many others, she had assumed that what she'd seen on television was true. "But mainly, the sheriff's department can't demand that anyone submit to DNA testing without just cause. And even then, it's iffy."

"Let's say it *was* someone who was young and desperate," Abby said, returning to the earlier supposition. "That might explain the makeshift diaper. If the baby was born on Sparrow Island, a new mom in this predicament—either resident or visitor—wouldn't have wanted to call attention to herself by shopping for baby things where she might be recognized."

"So maybe Moses was born on Orcas or one of the other

islands. Or perhaps on the mainland," Mary suggested. "Neil McDonald said that he wouldn't necessarily have noticed if someone had smuggled a baby aboard the ferry."

"I don't have any personal experience to back this up," Abby said, "but I can't imagine a mother making such a long crossing from the mainland so soon after giving birth. Besides, if the baby had come here from Seattle or farther away, the person or persons who brought Moses here would have had access to any number of stores where they could have bought supplies anonymously."

Henry nodded. "And who's to say they didn't come over from one of the other islands on a private boat? But as you said, they still could have bought diapers without being noticed. My own theory is that Moses was born right here and that the person who left him on the doorstep also lives here."

Mary set her teacup down on the end table. "Then that rules out teenagers. I talked to Janet tonight and she said that Margaret Blackstock over at the school hasn't seen any expectant girls. And she would have noticed."

There was no question about that. Between Janet and Margaret, they knew almost everything that happened on Sparrow Island. And to whom.

"The baby's mother could have been a homeschooled student," Abby suggested.

"Margaret knows those kids too." Mary straightened in her chair. "Homeschooling parents have to file their paperwork with the school," Mary continued. "None of those families has dark hair like Moses', and even if they did I'm sure their own parents would have noticed that their daughter was pregnant one day and not the next."

Mary's fidgeting, Abby had come to understand, could be

either an indication of excitement or fatigue. In this case, Abby suspected it was both.

As it turned out, fatigue was taking its toll on Henry too. He stood, prompting Finnegan to rise and circle his legs for attention. Henry scratched the top of the dog's bony head, then leaned back and stretched his arms.

"You two go ahead and chew on this awhile. If you figure out 'whodunit,' be sure to let me know," he said with a teasing grin. "Meanwhile, I'm going home to rest so I'll have energy to chase down some real clues tomorrow."

Abby couldn't help asking, "Such as?"

Henry paused with Mary's hand just inches from his lips. He kissed her knuckles, then gave them a gentle squeeze in his big hand before answering.

"We have a handwriting analyst looking over the note that was left with the baby," he began.

"But it was written in block letters," Mary said. "How can you analyze handwriting that's been intentionally altered?"

"Even squared-off letters reveal something about the person who wrote them," Henry responded. "We've sent the ink and stationery to be tested at the lab, but I strongly suspect they'll be ordinary ballpoint ink like that from a stick pen and computer paper that's sold in bulk at any office supply store. This person does not want to be found."

That might be so, but Abby knew the truth needed to come out even if mother and child were not ultimately reunited.

But a big part of the reason that Abby wanted this case solved was so that her own mother could find whatever peace she was searching for. It was important to Ellen that the child's mother be found, so Abby was committed to making sure they located her. "A mother needs to be with her baby," Ellen had said earlier this evening. "Or, if she truly wants to give him up for adoption, then she needs to say a proper good-bye."

Abby agreed. To do it the way the parent had done—abandoning the child on a doorstep—left so much unfinished business, both for the parents and for the baby.

Similarly, Abby had the odd feeling that once the baby's situation was resolved, Ellen would also find closure for her own feelings of unrest.

A renewed sense of determination filled Abby as she considered what needed to be done. Although she felt certain that God was calling her to become more involved to help uncover the truth behind this mystery, she would pray about it before bed tonight to make certain she was following His will.

And tomorrow she would start by making a visit to In Stitches to ask the owner, Ana Dominguez, a few questions.

AFTER HENRY HAD LEFT, Mary surprised Abby by announcing that she had been thinking about Hugo's suggestion to enter the Skills and Crafts walkathon.

"It's not because of anything that anyone said or did tonight," Mary was quick to point out. "In fact, everyone was very apologetic for having left me out of the walkathon planning meeting. They thought they'd been doing me a favor by not putting me in an uncomfortable position. But they understand now that it's better to ask and let me decide whether or not I want to participate."

"That's wonderful!" Abby stood and collected the cups to take them to the kitchen. "So there were no hurt or awkward feelings?"

"Nary a one. Before the meeting started, I pulled the leaders aside for a brief chat. I said that although I couldn't offer much help with the 'legwork,' so to speak, I was more than happy to offer a helping hand wherever else it was needed."

Mary grinned at her own pun, and once again, Abby was left to marvel at her sister's skill at smoothing over a potentially uncomfortable situation with grace, wit and charm. She followed Abby into the kitchen where Abby quickly washed the cups and saucers, then passed them to Mary to dry.

"After the opening prayer for the Skills and Crafts meeting, little Hillary Storm was assigned the job of passing out sponsor sheets," Mary continued. "As innocent as could be, she asked me if I wanted one."

Mary stacked the dried dishes on the counter for Abby to put in the cupboard.

"Well, wouldn't you know it, Bobby's eyes got big and he gave her a little kick."

Abby closed the cupboard door and sat at the table to hear the rest of Mary's story. "Aw, that's so sweet. He was being protective of you."

"Oh, I fully understood that his heart was in the right place," Mary agreed. "But it occurred to me that his thinking was limited as to what he believed I could and couldn't do. And if my little buddy thought this way, then what might the rest of the kids think?"

"So what did you do?" Abby hooked an elbow over the back of her chair and got comfortable. She loved it whenever Mary got on a crusade to impress an important point upon the children.

"Well, I explained that the Lord often uses people in ways that are not expected. Jacob, a man who walked with a limp, fathered a nation of God's people. Moses had a speech impediment, but the Lord used him as His spokesman. And Esther was an orphan, but God made her a Queen and she saved her people." Mary folded the tea towel that lay across her lap, then laid her hands on top of the tidy square. "I'm no Esther, but with my Father's help, I can certainly find a way to complete a 10K walkathon."

Abby smiled and leaned forward to clasp her sister's hands. "You always seem to know just the right thing to say."

"Believe me, I prayed and asked the Lord to put the right attitude in my heart and the right words in my mouth. Then I took that paper, pretty as you please, and wrote down Hugo Baron's name as my first sponsor. After that, I flexed my arms for the kids and told them they'd better start training because even though I can't outrun them, I can sure out-roll them."

Abby jumped from her chair to hug her sister. "Mary, that's wonderful! I knew you wouldn't let anything hold you back." She returned to her chair, perching on its edge. "Put my name in the number two spot on your sponsor form."

"Too late. After the meeting, each of the other leaders signed my sheet. But I'll add your John Hancock below theirs."

Despite Mary's satisfaction over having resolved the issue of being left out of the walkathon planning, something else was obviously troubling her. She pushed her chair back and, after wetting a cloth at the sink, busied herself with wiping the counters even though they didn't need it.

"Are you having second thoughts about doing this?" Abby asked. Although she had loved Hugo's idea that Mary enter the race, only Mary and the Lord knew if it was the right thing for her to do.

"Not second thoughts," Mary said, squeezing the cloth into

the sink. "Just thinking about Bobby's behavior this evening. I'm concerned that he might be cheating so he can win the contest for recruiting the most sponsors."

"What did he say?"

"It wasn't anything he said. It was what he *didn't* say." Mary placed the cloth over the faucet to dry. "He seemed very smug. It was as if he was pleased with himself for pulling one over on us."

"Perhaps you should talk to him. Ask a few questions to see what he's up to, then let him know where he's going wrong."

"I don't know if I should be the one to do that," Mary protested.

"Why not? He's a good kid and he respects you a lot. He'll listen to what you have to say."

"Thanks."

Abby stood and turned to head upstairs. Mary touched a hand to Abby's waist as she moved past her. Abby stopped and turned, her heart filling with love for the woman she was blessed to claim as her sister.

"Well, for what it's worth, I think the world of you."

CHAPTER ❧ SIX

On her return from the Thursday morning bird-watching outing to Cedar Grove Lake, Abby made her way through The Nature Museum toward her office. Wilma Washburn, a sixty-something Native American with gray hair that highlighted her coppery skin, sat at the reception desk where she greeted visitors with her usual friendly attitude. Wilma nodded briefly to Abby before answering a child's request for directions to the bathroom.

Scattered from strategic points in the reception area, realistic looking birds hung suspended from the ceiling where they seemed as though they were about to dive toward the wall displays that advertised the museum's latest events. One of the displays was clearly a work in progress, and its creator stepped back to get a broader view of what he had accomplished so far.

Abby smiled as the Curator of the museum stepped back and adjusted his blue silk tie. She stepped closer and mimicked Hugo's pose, one arm folded over her chest and the other hand tapping her chin.

"Looks good," she said.

The bulletin board's purpose was to promote the upcoming feature film for children that taught the various forms of travel for animals. One panel showed a myna bird piloting an airplane, another featured a salamander wearing a superhero cape as it climbed up the side of a large rock, and the third depicted a harbor seal gliding through the water in a cartoon-like submarine.

"It's missing something." Hugo moved a couple of the characters around on the display, but it still seemed very two-dimensional.

Abby looked closer and had to agree with him. The display intentionally lacked the sophistication of some of the other exhibits, as the bright colors and simple art were intended to appeal to younger children. However, it needed something else. Something to give it the illusion of depth.

"Have you asked Wilma what she thinks? She's pretty creative with this sort of thing."

"It needs a better backdrop," Wilma volunteered from her station at the reception desk. "The plain colors up there now don't add much to the overall effect."

As swiftly as she'd entered their conversation, Wilma turned away to pull out a brochure for an elderly visitor who was interested in the whale exhibit.

Hugo backed away another step. "Agreed, but I just don't see how to remedy it. I'm better at dreaming up the ideas," he said, "and hiring smart people to carry them through."

His words were meant for both women and he backed them up with a pleasant wink. He was being playful, and Abby wanted to respond with something pithy and clever such as Katharine Hepburn might have said in one of her classic movies from the 1940s and '50s. But the perfect repartee eluded her.

Instead, she said, "I wouldn't worry about it if I were you. Creating display boards is something that can be learned, but creating relationships is something that comes naturally to you."

Hugo grinned and turned away from his not-quite-there display to face Abby. "I wasn't able to make it to the Skills and Crafts meeting last night, but I take it Mary decided to enter the walkathon as I suggested?"

"Yes, and everything's all smoothed over with the other leaders."

"Excellent!" he said, giving himself a verbal pat on the back. But then he must have noticed the flicker of concern that had come rushing back to Abby. He gently goaded her to reveal what was bothering her. "However . . . ?"

"Right now, she's more concerned that Bobby's lost sight of the goal to help our sister church on the mainland."

Abby filled Hugo in, explaining that their young friend had been acting peculiar about his list of sponsors. "Ordinarily I wouldn't have brought it up at all, especially since we don't know for certain if there's any cheating going on," she said. "But since you're a Skills and Crafts mentor whom all the children look up to, I thought you might give him some subtle guidance in playing by the rules."

"I'd be happy to help steer our little friend to the high road," he offered.

"Thanks. I knew you'd understand." Abby pulled the digital camera out of her birding pouch. For informal bird-watching such as she did on outings with casual hobbyists, she used the digital camera so she could upload the photos to the Web site or use them for The Nature Museum's displays. The traditional film camera came out whenever a rare bird was spotted. In Abby's opinion, the old-fashioned film lent authenticity to the photos since they were not as easily altered as those taken with newer technology.

"Catch any good images today?" Hugo sidled closer to squint at the two-inch screen on the back of her camera.

Sometimes it seemed as though Hugo was as excited about the birds that winged their way past Abby's viewfinder as she was. No matter how many times she went birding or how many different images she captured of the same kinds of birds, he always wanted to see what she'd brought back. It was a nice way to enjoy the excursion all over again, only this time his observant or funny commentaries added a rich new layer to the experience.

"There are a few really good ones," she said, pressing the button to scroll through the pictures. "I like this one of two common terns in midair fighting over a herring."

"Excellent! You can even see the water droplets spraying off the fish."

His arm brushed hers, momentarily distracting Abby from the colorful images flashing across the tiny screen. She took a breath and refocused her attention.

"One of the birders mentioned having seen a loggerhead shrike," she said significantly.

Hugo leaned closer, obviously excited by this rare news. "There've never been any proven sightings of the loggerhead on Sparrow Island. Did you get a picture?"

"No, and none of the rest of us saw it." If that had actually been what Conrad had seen, the black-masked *butcher bird*, as it was commonly known, should have been easy to spot since the little hunter liked to perch in the open to watch for prey.

"Perhaps it was a northern shrike," Hugo suggested. "They're occasionally seen around here."

"That's not very likely since they've never been reported during the summer. Besides, none of us saw evidence of its kills."

The robin-sized shrikes were known for their tendency to cache the bodies of their prey by impaling them upon a plant spike and hoarding them for dining later. If anyone had come near one of those stashes, the feisty shrike of either variety would have made itself known by aggressively defending its larder.

"What about a northern mockingbird?" Hugo asked. "They can be mistaken for a shrike if one only gets a quick glimpse."

Abby nodded and looked down at the western tanager she'd managed to capture, thanks to a long-distance lens and her walking stick that converted to a steady tripod on which to rest her camera. The brightly colored male, with his red head and yellow breast, had been elusive in his perch high up in the forest canopy. But his distinct *pit-ur-tuc* call had alerted Abby to his presence, after which she'd challenged the bird-watchers to find the tropical-colored bird.

Most of them had been able to spot the nearly hidden tanager, but only one of their group had seen the less bashful shrike, as the loggerhead was also known.

"If Conrad spotted a shrike," she said, "he was either very lucky or very mistaken." Abby didn't bother to voice the third option. That the creature he'd drawn in his sketchbook had not been the rendering of a real bird but perhaps copied from the guidebook that he carried with him. "I want it to be a true sighting, but something tells me luck wasn't necessarily with him today."

"But if luck was with him," Hugo persisted, "you'll need to

report it to the birding society. They'd want to know if either of the shrikes is making an appearance here."

"Right. I'm going to try to verify it before filing the report."

Hugo still peered at the view screen as Abby flipped back through the pictures until she came to some that had been taken earlier in the week. She hit the *Off* button and moved to put the camera back in her birding bag.

"Wait, what was that?" Hugo reached for the camera.

Turning it back on, she handed it to him. "They're just the pictures I snapped of baby Moses before Mom and I took him to the Medical Center. Henry kept the basket and all the other stuff as evidence, so he doesn't need my photos."

"*Mmm-hmmm.*" Although Hugo didn't need glasses, he squinted a bit to make out the details of the pixilated image. "Wilma," he said, moving toward the reception desk. "This basket reminds me of your artwork. Would you happen to know anything about it?"

Wilma prided herself on having kept alive the basket-weaving skills she'd learned from her grandmother. One time she had commented that it seemed like she was keeping a part of her grandmother alive whenever she finished a new piece. She said she imagined her grandmother's love of handcrafted beauty touching the lives of the customers who bought the pieces at Bayside Souvenirs or Island Blooms.

The receptionist leaned against the counter and frowned at the small image. "Yes, that's one of mine. I like to make my picnic baskets long and shallow like that so you can see everything at once. And even if I didn't recognize the basketry, I certainly remember the liner in there. It's deep blue with little white lightning bolts on it." As an afterthought, she added, "With all that black hair, he almost looks Native American like me, doesn't he?"

"Dr. Randolph said he's Caucasian, but I wonder how you'd know something like that for sure." Abby zoomed the picture to get a better look at the basket liner and, sure enough, there were cheerful little bolts zapping in all directions.

"See?" Wilma jabbed a tanned finger at the screen. "Ana Dominguez special ordered the fabric for me so I could use it for baskets to sell during the Flashback Festival. Get it? *Flash*-back."

Hugo chuckled politely, but Abby's thoughts had flashed back to last fall. The festival was held around the third week of September every year. And, given the date of Moses' birth, he must have been conceived no later than early October. The connection eluded her now, but she was determined to track this basket back to the person who'd bought it. Perhaps that information would direct her toward the person who'd left that precious little child on the Senior Center's doorstep.

"I assume you didn't sell these through Mary's flower shop?" she asked.

"Oh no. Mary prefers the smaller baskets for her arrangements. I only made three of these picnic baskets and they were all sold through Bayside Souvenirs." She tapped her finger on the counter. "Come to think of it, only two of them sold during the week of the festival. I was beginning to think I'd have to take back the third one since few people want to buy picnic baskets in October. It sure surprised me when that third one was snapped up too. I wondered if I should have made more."

"Interesting."

Abby was aware that Hugo was eyeing her speculatively.

He'd known her long enough to tell when she was hot on the trail of clues. And this was one of those times.

She was about to ask him for an extra-long lunchtime to check out these new leads when Wilma asked her to zoom in on the beach towel that covered the baby.

"Blue was a popular color last year. Donna Morgan over at Bayside Souvenirs stocked those towels because she said tourists wanted something to remind them of Sparrow Island. The two white sails superimposed over the blue background makes people think of the boats on Randolph Bay."

Abby adjusted the picture in the frame to get a closer look at the white corner of the sail Wilma had pointed out. That was when her attention fell on the handkerchief bonnet that covered the baby's head.

Some people referred to them as baptism or christening bonnets, but those were usually a bit more frilly than this one. This particular head covering, bordered only by a simple edging of blue thread, indicated that it had probably been made from a man's handkerchief. At the front corners, pale blue ribbons had been attached with a pale blue thread that matched the border, but an extra little touch had been added in the form of three small eyelets, also edged in blue.

Thank goodness the camera had fantastic clarity. Abby zoomed in again, this time enlarging the corner of the bonnet to fill the screen.

"That's good workmanship," Wilma commented. "Somebody's very handy with the needle." She reached for the camera and tilted it toward her for a better look. "I've seen that ribbon at In Stitches. Maybe Ana could help you narrow down who bought it."

"That's not all that's at In Stitches," Abby said, remembering the bolts of print fabrics that Mary had bought for a recent Skills and Crafts project. With a smile at her boss, she said, "Ana has the perfect material for the backdrops of your display. If you'd like, I could pop over there and save you the trouble."

Hugo hooked his thumbs over the suspenders that he wore more for style than function. With a knowing grin, he said, "Thank you for your generous offer. And since you're an excellent multitasker, I expect you'll be investigating that blue ribbon while you're there."

"That's a great idea!" Abby said as if she hadn't already thought of it. She tucked the camera back into her bag and hitched the strap up on her shoulder. "While I'm out, I'll probably multitask myself over to Bayside Souvenirs, too."

EVERY TIME ABBY walked into In Stitches, it felt like she was stepping back to a time when ladies made all the clothes, quilts and curtains for their families and homes. But despite the retro sense of overstuffed coziness in the shop, it also held some exciting modern touches such as various needlework and jewelry kits. And for sale in the far corner of the shop sat a couple of the latest sewing machines, one sporting an assortment of fancy stitch options and the other capable of connecting to a computer and automatically embroidering pre-programmed designs. No one had bought the computer-capable sewing machine yet, but every so often Ana would use it to demonstrate some fancy option it offered or even just to jazz up her own works in progress. Ana would never use a machine on the natural wall hangings she made and sold on the Internet, but she wasn't above taking a shortcut or two when whipping together a new peasant blouse with bright floral embroidery to decorate the bodice.

Today Ida Tolliver must have been off from the lunch shift at the Springhouse Café. She stood by the checkout counter with Ana, sorting through the driftwood, stones, feathers and bits of madrone bark they'd collected on their scavenger hunt this morning. These pieces would be used in Ana's wall hangings or perhaps given to Ana's husband Juan to make Mexican sculptures in his spare time after his nursing shifts were over.

As Abby entered the shop, the two women raised their heads from the pile of nature's baubles on the counter, but Abby gestured for them to continue their work while she browsed through the store.

It didn't take her long to find what she was looking for. The bolts of fabric sat conveniently close to the corner of the store usually reserved for the Busy Bee Quilting Society. She bypassed the brilliantly colored floral designs that Mary would have pulled out to admire if she'd been here. Instead, she focused on an underwater design, complete with images of sea grass, schools of fish and a grumpy looking crab. This would be the perfect backdrop for Hugo's harbor seal in the submarine.

A simple blue fabric dotted with white clouds would do for the myna bird in the airplane, and a forest print would work nicely to showcase the gravity-defying salamander.

Abby set the bolts down on one of the empty Busy Bee chairs and looked through the assortment of ribbons and rickrack trim. As she pulled her camera out to compare the bonnet ribbon with that on the shelf, she overheard Ida talking about her latest interest.

"It's the hot, new thing. All the people my age are doing it. I'm making an afghan to go on the back of my sofa. Who knew that knitting could be so much fun?"

Abby looked up in time to catch the look of amusement on

Ana's face. The store owner unhooked and refastened the clasp that held her salt-and-pepper hair behind her shoulders.

"Imagine that," Ana said with a gentle teasing tone as she cleared the counter of their bounty. "I'll be sure to let my crafting group know so they can be on the cutting edge."

Ida seemed not to catch the humorous irony in Ana's statement. "Knitting's very relaxing," she continued as if she were imparting new information. "That's why the twenty-somethings like it so much. It helps us deal with the stress of our quarter-life crises."

Abby picked up a roll of the blue ribbon and took it along with the fabric to the front of the store for Ana to measure and cut.

The pretty Mexican woman's hands flew swiftly as she marked, cut and folded the material. Rather than measure the cloth with a tape measure, she merely gauged the distance from her elbow to fingertips. Abby had no doubt it would be very close to or slightly longer than the amount she had requested.

"As it turns out," Ana said, continuing the conversation she'd been having with Ida, "the midlife crisis set and the three-quarterlifers have also been busy at work with their knitting. Miss Opal Collins has already made a beautiful blanket for the *bebè*, and Harriet Travis is working on a pair of booties." With a wink to Abby, she added, "Even the original Moses, living in the pharaoh's house, never had so many clothes and *mantas* as the ladies at the Senior Center are making for your mother's little visitor."

Ida had picked up a couple of skeins of variegated yarn and now toyed with them as she leaned one elbow against the counter. "How are Ellen and George doing with a little baby in the house?"

"They're tired," Abby said, summing up the conversation she'd had with her mother recently. "When I called her a few minutes ago, she said she was on her way to The Green Grocer to try a different brand of formula. Moses cried a bit last night and Dr. Randolph thinks he may have a touch of colic."

Ana shook her head. "My family believes in feeding *bebès* the milk that God gives mothers. Then if he had colic, you would just change the mother's diet." She paused a moment. "But in Ellen's case, I suppose that would be hard to do."

Abby grinned. "She loves taking care of the baby, but I suppose she'd draw the line at that."

"I saw your dad at the restaurant last night," Ida said. "He was getting takeout for two because your mom hasn't had time to cook."

"That rascal! I told him I'd come over and fix dinner for them, but he insisted he had everything under control."

Ida laughed. "Yeah, he said you'd offered, but he had a hankering for a Springhouse steak." She set the skeins of yarn back in the display bin. "He was like a proud grandpa flashing pictures of Moses around for everyone to see."

"They seem to be getting really attached to the baby," Abby said.

Ana bagged her purchase, but didn't bother to finish the sale. Obviously, she was used to a lot of last-minute impulse purchases, so she allowed time for the whim to strike. Either that or she'd noticed the spool of ribbon in Abby's hand.

"Terza Choi is just as bad," Ana said. "She's been at the Stanton Farm every day since the baby came to stay with Ellen."

"Who's running the bed-and-breakfast?" Ida asked.

"Martin's picking up her share of the duties," Ana said,

turning her attention back to her young friend. "But he doesn't seem to mind. He even *encourages* her to go over there and help Ellen."

That explained why Abby hadn't seen much of the woman when she'd transported the birders back and forth to The Bird Nest each day. But why would Martin encourage his wife to take time away from the bed-and-breakfast during their busiest season? It didn't make sense.

One thing was certain, though. "It sure has lifted my mother's spirits to be taking care of the baby," Abby said. "And Terza has been a tremendous help and a calming influence for both of them."

Ana's cocoa-brown eyes darkened. "I worry about when the baby goes."

"Me too." Abby laid the ribbon on the counter, then fished the camera out of her bag. "That's why I need your help."

Ida sidled closer to see what was unfolding. The twenty-four-year-old fancied herself a Watson to Abby's Sherlock Holmes and loved to get involved in whatever adventures came Abby's way.

"Whatever I can do, you can count on me," Ana promised.

Abby showed them both the pictures on her camera. She hadn't taken the time to print them out, but the digital version would show enough to spark recognition if either of the women had seen the samples of evidence before.

"That's one of Wilma Washburn's baskets," Ana said. "She bought that liner fabric here to tie in with the Flashback Festival theme. I told her people wouldn't get the connection with lightning, but she wouldn't listen to me."

Ida nodded her agreement. "It makes me think of a sudden storm washing out a picnic."

"And I've seen that beach towel before, but I can't remember where."

That was no problem since Wilma had already pointed her to the Bayside Souvenir shop.

"What about the other items?" Abby asked as she flipped through the photos of the ribbon, the bonnet and the dishtowel diaper. "It looks like the ribbon came from here, but do any of the other things look familiar?"

Ana picked up a small magnifying glass that hung from a cord around her neck. Holding it over the photo of the bonnet, she compared it with the ribbon on the counter.

"Yes, that's my ribbon. That's one of my best sellers. People use it for everything from quilting to little girls' dresses to wrapping small packages."

Abby tapped a finger to her chin. "So it would be out of the question for you to tell me who might have bought this ribbon?"

"Sure, I can tell you who bought it."

Ida looked surprised, and Abby felt a surge of hope.

"Everybody." Ana let the magnifying glass drop back to her chest. "Everybody and their aunt and grandmother and sister. Too many to count."

Air came whooshing out of Abby's lungs like a deflated balloon. "That's what I was afraid of."

"I love the bonnet, though," Ana offered.

"Me too," Ida said as if she were afraid of being left out. "It's really simple but cute."

"That tea towel that Moses is wearing as a diaper. It's used," Ana said with conviction.

Abby frowned at the screen. "Actually, he was still dry when I took this picture."

"No, I mean it was used to dry dishes before someone

turned it into a diaper. See? There's some fraying on the cloth near his tummy."

Abby hadn't had much hope for tracking down the makeshift diaper since it seemed to be the consensus that it was most likely a mass-produced item purchased at a discount store on the mainland. "Okay, so the trail on the dish towel is stale. May as well forget about that for now."

"Not so quick, *mi amiga*." Ana tilted the camera for another look. "It could have been part of a set. If you find the matching towel or dish cloth, then you are a step closer to the *madre*."

Right. She'd be like Prince Charming trying to match a glass slipper to the right foot. Only in Abby's case, she'd have to go into the kitchen of every house on Sparrow Island looking for the match to an inexpensively made towel.

The door opened and a couple of women walked in clutching needlepoint pattern books.

"Do you want that ribbon?" Ana asked, preparing to conclude the sale.

Abby paused for a moment, but decided that she'd found out all she could about the ribbon for now. Next on her to-do list was a visit to Bayside Souvenirs. Then it was back to Cedar Grove Lake to look for what was probably a nonexistent loggerhead shrike.

"No, the fabric is all I need."

Ana rang up the sale, then counted back the change from the money Abby had given her.

"If you find out who made that bonnet, send them my way," she said, handing the bag to Abby. "The Busy Bees would love to learn that eyelet stitch."

CHAPTER ✤ SEVEN

Ellen lifted the fidgety baby out of the built-in infant seat on the shopping cart and raised him to her shoulder while Terza dashed over to the next aisle to pick up some laundry detergent. She had arrived at the farm as George was preparing to drive Ellen to The Green Grocer, so he'd naturally invited Terza to ride along with them.

"*Shhh*," Ellen said as she gently jiggled Moses in her arms. He wasn't crying yet, just fussing, but judging from the way he'd acted last night, she guessed he was gearing up for another squall-fest.

Aside from her great-grandchildren's visits from Florida, it had been a long time since Ellen had taken her cart up the baby aisle at The Green Grocer. She couldn't believe how many different kinds of baby formula were available nowadays. Moving to one side, she searched for the brand Dr. Randolph had recommended.

After a long fretful night with the baby, they'd called the doctor for advice. Dr. Randolph had readily diagnosed the trouble as colic and suggested a change of formula to help ease the baby's tummy distress.

With that in mind, George had brought Ellen to the grocery store right away. She had assured him that she'd be fine with Terza for support while in the store, so he had dashed off to the nearby library to find a book on early infant child care. Though they'd both had plenty of experience taking care of their own children and grandchildren, they decided after last night's colic episode that they needed a refresher.

"Oh my, what a cutie," someone said softly behind her.

Ellen turned and was pleasantly surprised to find Tamara Preston stroking the baby's arm. Her own cart, containing potato chips, personal products, a large bottle of aspirin, several frozen dinners and a package of "Skinny Mini" meal replacement bars, indicated that she could use some help in the meal planning department.

"Goodness, I was so absorbed in the baby formula that I didn't even hear you come up. How are you doing, dear?"

"That's what I should be asking you," the young woman said. "You certainly have your hands full."

"Would you like to hold him?"

Tamara hesitated and actually took a step back. Ellen understood her reluctance. In her volunteer position at the Senior Center, Tamara was used to helping some of the older folks maneuver around, but she probably didn't have much experience handling a tiny infant.

"It's okay. You don't have to if you're not comfortable."

She flipped her blonde hair behind her shoulder and seemed to be giving the situation a lot of thought. "It's not that I don't want to. Really."

Taking great care to support the baby's head, Ellen transferred him to her other arm. Tamara watched the child with wholehearted interest, despite her reluctance to hold him. "That's okay. It's better to say no when you're unsure than to take a chance on dropping him."

"He's a terrific little guy, isn't he?" Tamara asked. "I wonder who's going to adopt him."

"There are lots of people in the San Juan Islands and on the mainland who want him." After the news had hit the Seattle newspapers and television stations, people had come out of the woodwork to ask to adopt the baby. Couples, singles, even a few in their fifties or older . . . they all wanted to take this darling child and raise him.

But Tamara seemed not to have heard her. "If we had a baby in the house," she said, gently stroking the boy's dark hair, "maybe Pete wouldn't work so much overtime."

Ellen reached for a can of formula and put it in the cart. Whatever was going on between Tamara and her husband was between them and God. It wasn't her place to butt in and tell Tamara how to handle her marriage.

But then, as if it had been whispered to her, something brought to mind the message in Titus 2:3. Ellen couldn't recall all of it, not the way Abby was able to remember her Bible, but she recalled that it said something about older women training the younger ones to love their husbands and children.

"A baby is a blessing," Ellen agreed, "but it can't heal problems in a marriage. It wouldn't be fair to expect that of a child."

"I know. You're completely right. And I didn't mean to complain about Pete. It's just that he travels so much, and . . . well . . . I miss him." The baby squirmed in Ellen's arms, and

Tamara automatically took a half step away, as if her mere presence might have caused him to fidget. "Pete just got home on Tuesday, but he'll be leaving in a few days for his next sales trip."

Tamara's experience brought back long-ago memories of her own sweetheart being away for long periods of time. "When I met George, he was in the Navy," Ellen said. "It was exciting at first, writing to him and keeping up a long-distance relationship. And I was proud of him for working so hard and trying to make a positive impact for our nation. The homecomings were always so sweet. But it usually turned sad when he got his orders for his next assignment."

"I know what you mean. Pete sells and installs state-of-the-art medical equipment all over North America. Because of him, lives are being saved. So I feel guilty for wanting him to stay home with me."

"God created us to be social creatures. We're supposed to turn to each other for love and companionship." Ellen pushed Tamara's cart to one side to make room for another shopper to pass by. "So He certainly understands our loneliness at times. Have you tried to work out a compromise so that both of you can get what you need from each other?"

Tamara nodded and a blonde curl bounced against her cheek.

Moses lifted his head, then abruptly dropped his face to Ellen's shoulder.

"That's why I started volunteering at the Senior Center," Tamara said. "To stay busy so I wouldn't miss Pete so much and help others at the same time."

"That's a good start."

"Unfortunately, Pete didn't want to give up the overtime

because he says that's the only way to become his company's top salesman."

Ellen tilted her head to one side, trying to understand why a man as nice as her husband wouldn't give a little on this matter.

Tamara must have noticed her confusion, for she quickly added, "You see, he's trying to save up enough money before we start a family so our children won't ever want for anything."

She went on to explain that he'd first been aiming for a five-figure sum that would cover purchasing all the furniture, clothes, diapers and other things they'd need to prepare for a child.

"We've got that covered now, plus some," she said with a sigh. "But then after he read how much it's going to cost to send a kid to college in twenty years, he freaked out and decided that now we need a much larger savings account before we can even think of adding another member to our family."

Ellen was glad the Prestons were taking the responsibilities of parenthood seriously, but she couldn't help wondering if perhaps Pete was going a little overboard in his zeal to be financially prepared. At some point, after a couple has made every reasonable preparation to bring a child into the world, it is then time to turn the matter over to God and trust Him to take care of the rest.

"Perhaps you can get some outside help to try to reach a fair compromise," Ellen suggested. "It says in the Bible that it's wise to seek out trusted advisers when necessary."

"That's why we're seeing Rev. Hale," Tamara confessed. "We just had our first counseling session last night. We'll have to schedule the rest of them around Pete's travels."

Ellen had been thinking along the lines of a financial adviser, but their solution was an even better start to solve their differing approaches toward their common goal.

Moses wiggled in Ellen's arms and pulled his knees up under his tummy. Ellen had a solid grasp of the squirming child, so she just focused on trying to make him comfortable.

Tamara watched, carefully studying Ellen's every movement. "I think we can be good parents once we get past the problem of Pete's work schedule."

Ellen said nothing, but reached for a bottle of lotion and added it to her cart.

"I think I'll be a good mom someday," Tamara said, lifting a hand to the shelf to tentatively touch a package of newborn diapers. "You've seen me at the Senior Center. I have a good work ethic and I'm nice to people even when they're having a bad day. Those are good qualities for raising a child."

Ellen immediately recalled the time that Thelma Rogers had scolded Tamara for treating her "like an old lady" merely because she'd offered to assist her up the rain-slick steps of the Senior Center. Despite Tamara's surprise at the unwarranted rebuke, she had politely apologized and continued on with her duties at the center.

"Of course you'll make a good mom. You definitely have the nurturing gene." Ellen was about to say more words of encouragement, but Moses chose that moment to crank up and start crying.

She jiggled harder, but that didn't make any difference in the decibel level. "It's colic," Ellen said as she patted the child's back. "There's not much anyone can do when a baby gets a tummy bubble."

Tamara seemed filled with sympathy, for Ellen and especially for Moses. She gripped the cart handle and with a halfhearted good-bye started off down the aisle. But before she'd gone very far, she stopped and called out over the baby's crying, "There's a box of handmade stuff for Moses at the Senior Center. When you weren't available to lead this week's recipe trading project, Emma Stoltz suggested that everyone make sock dolls and bibs for the baby."

"How sweet. I'll ask George to stop by there later and pick them up."

When Tamara turned away that time, Ellen could have sworn there were tears in her eyes.

Ellen needed to get out of the store soon, before Moses' cries broke the glass windows at the front of the store. She reached into the tote bag she'd brought with her and withdrew a pacifier. The gift from Mary depicted a goofy, one-toothed grin on the part that covered the baby's mouth. It had made them all laugh. Ellen popped the calming contraption into Moses' mouth and almost instantly, he quieted down. But Ellen suspected this was only a temporary fix.

"What's wrong with her?" Terza asked, as she returned with a jug of detergent and placed it in the basket. She gestured in the direction Tamara had gone. "It looked like she was crying."

Ellen paused before answering. Terza had been a wonderful friend this week and she had enjoyed getting to know her better during the time they'd spent together. But no matter how close they'd become, Ellen felt it necessary to guard Tamara's privacy about the marital problem she'd just shared. So Ellen came up with a vague explanation for why she looked a little rattled.

"Maybe she thinks her biological clock is ticking."

"Hers and those bird ladies'," Terza said as she chucked the baby's chin and grinned at the silly expression painted on the pacifier. "Jenny Hunsicker's college friend came to visit her for a couple of weeks, but they had a disagreement over which one of them should adopt Moses. Now the friend is so upset, she moved to The Bird Nest for the rest of her vacation."

Ellen took a chance that Moses had calmed enough to put him back into the baby carrier. But as soon as she laid him down, his face reddened and he drew up his legs. "It's a shame that people are being so competitive about a matter that they should be taking to the Lord."

"Yes, he definitely has colic," Terza said, picking the child up out of the carrier. Once she settled him against her chest, he immediately calmed down.

"Dr. Randolph suggested we change his formula to see if that helps."

"It won't hurt, but I have something else that will help," the tiny woman said knowingly. "Follow me."

Left with no other option, Ellen obediently followed her friend past the pastas and canned goods to a well stocked row of spices.

Terza tilted her head back to see the print on the bottles then plucked one off the shelf and handed it to Ellen. "It's not fresh, but it will do."

At the Chinese woman's request—no, insistence—Archie Goodfellow, the store owner had reluctantly begun stocking a limited quantity of her native produce. Although Terza was proficient at cooking American meals for her guests, she sometimes created Chinese dishes for those who wanted an authentic Chinese meal. After Archie had grumpily predicted that the fresh bok choy and ginger root she wanted him to provide would go to waste, Terza had allowed herself a brief moment of back-patting after the first shipment had sold out within a couple of days.

Even so, Archie drew the line at carrying some of the more obscure fresh herbs she'd requested. So once every month or two, either she or Martin would take a trip to Seattle to visit an Asian grocery store. Then she'd cook their favorite dishes, sometimes bringing heaping platters of dumplings, lettuce wraps or mango pudding to the potluck suppers at Little Flock Church.

Ellen took the bottle that Terza held out to her. "Fennel seeds. I use these when I make sausage."

"Now you will make tea," she said. "Put a half teaspoon of crushed seeds in a cup of boiling water. Let it sit for about ten minutes, then strain it through cheesecloth to get the seeds out. After the water cools, give some to him in a bottle."

"Are you sure?" Ellen asked, putting the jar in her cart.

"That's what we did in China," Terza assured her. "He'll like it. Tastes like licorice. Best of all, it helps the air to pass."

She handed the baby back to Ellen and continued with her instructions.

"Then give him a bath in lavender water to help him relax. After that, wrap the blanket snug around him so he feels like he's still in his mama's belly. When you put him to bed, turn a fan on in the room to make a shushing noise."

Moses was tuning up to cry again, so Ellen adjusted the pacifier in his mouth. She hoped she'd remember all of these suggestions after she returned home. "Those are good ideas."

"One more," Terza said. "Make a . . ." She paused and rocked her arms in front of her waist as she groped for the right word. "A sling. Put him in it so he's close to your body. He wants to hear your heart." She smiled significantly. "Your walking around will help the air move through him. And no more colic!"

"Thank you so much," Ellen said. "Maybe I'll ask Abby to take turns with George and me carrying Moses in the sling."

Terza waved a hand in the air. "No need for that. I will help."

"But you've already done so much. I feel guilty for imposing on you so much."

"It's no bother," Terza insisted, her gaze clouding over as her thoughts apparently went elsewhere. "I need to spend time with the baby."

Ellen was about to ask her what she meant by that, but Moses wound up again and let loose with a blood-curdling cry. Fortunately, George showed up in the nick of time to whisk them through the checkout line and take them all home.

Although she was curious about the reason behind Terza's insistence on helping with the baby this week, Ellen would not ask her. After all, she had her own very personal reason for needing to take care of Moses.

THE FIRST THING Abby noticed when she walked into Bayside Souvenirs was the beach towel hanging from the wall near the back of the shop. It was just like the one that had been wrapped around Moses, but the background color of this one was green instead of blue.

Always ready to encourage a sale, Donna Morgan the shop manager noticed her interest and began telling her why she should buy the towel. "That's one of our best sellers. Green's the 'in' color this year."

"I'm not here to buy a towel," Abby said. "But if you have some handkerchiefs, I'd like to see them."

"Sure! Right over here." Donna led her to a table filled with small wooden chests, necklaces made of seashells, and paper fans illustrated with watercolor-style paintings of various birds. She picked up a set of three lacy handkerchiefs that had been rolled and tied with a pale green ribbon. "Kind of late for Mother's Day, isn't it?"

Although bubbly and personable, the forty-something blonde often had trouble containing her curiosity. Even worse, if one should share any information with her, Donna had trouble containing that too.

Well, it wasn't any secret that Abby was trying to find out who'd left little Moses at the Senior Center. So she didn't mind explaining to Donna her sudden interest in tourist gift items.

"Actually, I was looking for a man's handkerchief with a narrow blue trim around the border," Abby said. She didn't bother to pull out her camera this time since she needed to hurry out of here and get back to work. Seeing the speculation in Donna's eyes, she added, "The bonnet that Moses was wearing was made out of a handkerchief like that."

"Oh, I'm sorry. We don't carry men's handkerchiefs."

She looked so disappointed at not having supplied one of the clues to the baby's identity that Abby hoped her next question would give them both an opportunity for success.

"That's okay. What I really wanted to ask you about was a picnic basket made by Wilma Washburn."

"Bummer, I can't help you there either. We're all out." She returned the handkerchiefs to the table and straightened the boxes so they sat in a neat row. "Those picnic baskets are pretty pricey, but the tourists love them, so they go fast. Wilma tells me she'll have a couple more ready by the end of next week."

"I'm not here to buy one," Abby explained. "I was wondering if you could tell me about a basket you sold last fall, after the Flashback Festival."

"Oh yes, they were really cute, with the lightning bolts on the cloth inside." Donna put a hand on her slim hip. "It was so clever how Wilma used the little flashes to represent the Flashback Festival."

Great! She remembered them. Abby prayed that it wasn't too much to ask that Donna also remembered the person who'd bought the basket Moses had later lain in. "I know you have a lot of customers in here all the time, but do you happen to remember who bought them?"

"Strangely enough, I do. Mainly because the first one went so fast . . . just hours after Wilma brought them in. Harriet Travis wanted one for her knitting yarns. Said she was tired of her cat pulling the skeins out of her open tote bag. She was hoping the double lids would keep the yarns out of sight and out of mind."

It was not likely that Harriet Travis had taken the baby to the Senior Center, so Abby mentally crossed that particular basket off the list.

"Then, sometime during the Flashback Festival, a young woman—a tourist—bought the second one."

Abby reached into her bag for the notepad she always carried with her. This one had possibilities. "Do you recall what she looked like?"

If she had black hair, perhaps she was the mother of baby Moses.

"No. That, I don't recall. But I do remember her saying that her parents were about to celebrate their silver anniversary. The girl didn't want the hassle of taking the basket home on the ferry, so she asked me to wrap it up and mail it to her parents." Donna smiled as if quite pleased with herself. "I suggested that instead of giving the couple an empty basket, she should fill it with something nice. So I was able to up-sell a set of souvenir salt and pepper shakers, a Sparrow Island umbrella because you can always count on it to rain during a picnic, a set of unbreakable dishes and a bud vase."

"Wow, what a romantic gift." Abby would have to remember that as a possible gift in the future . . . perhaps when or if Mary and Henry ever decided to get married.

"That's not all. For the finishing touch, I ordered a pair of wine glasses and a lacy tablecloth from Winifred's. They've been good about sending their customers to my store, so it was nice to be able to reciprocate."

Winifred's was the most upscale restaurant in Green Harbor, and possibly even in the entire San Juan Islands. So their contribution to the anniversary basket would have definitely added an elegant touch.

It didn't seem likely, but Abby supposed that if the girl's parents lived nearby, she might have borrowed back the gift and used it during her time of desperation.

"It's not the kind of gift that people in South Carolina see every day," Donna bragged.

That answered that. Abby persisted, hoping that she'd find the answers she needed from the next one. "I understand there were three baskets that Wilma had made with the lightning bolt liner."

"Yeah, I was beginning to wonder if that third one would sell before the end of the tourist season." By now Donna had moved to the rack of swimsuits and beach cover-ups and was grouping them by color. "I hate to carry over a lot of inventory from one year to the next."

"But it did sell," Abby prompted, remembering what Wilma had told her earlier.

Donna nodded and moved the size two suit to the front of the rack. "Right. Some guy came in shortly after the Flashback Festival was over, looking to buy something for the sweetie he'd met here during the festival. When he saw the basket, he decided a romantic picnic was the way to go."

"In October?" Although the weather in the San Juans remained quite moderate throughout the year, autumn was still a bit chilly to be eating outside.

"That's what I thought. But he just said they'd make it an indoor picnic in front of the fireplace." She continued moving through the store, with Abby staying close by as she folded and repositioned the merchandise. "I tried the up-selling thing with him, too, but he didn't want to go all out, the way that girl did for her parents' anniversary. Maybe because it was for someone he'd only just met. However, I did sell him one of those beach towels to use as a picnic cloth on the floor."

"Interesting. He didn't happen to mention who his love interest was, did he?"

"No, he just said he was going to the Springhouse Café to buy a couple of steak dinners. A nice, juicy Springhouse steak is great, but if he'd really wanted to impress her, he should have followed my advice and ordered the meals from Winifred's." Donna stopped straightening the merchandise for a moment and turned to face Abby. "Do you think this guy was the father of Moses Doe?"

Abby gave it some thought and once again calculated the months. "If so, probably not until after the romantic picnic," she said significantly. It seemed as though they were getting close. Now if only Donna could give her enough specifics to track him down. "Can you tell me a little more about this man?"

"The majority of the tourists who come through here all blur together because the young people are usually dressed for the beach, and the older ones tend to go for a more conservative, yet casual style." She pushed a hand through her hair as she thought back to last October. "This guy fit a different mold. He was in his early forties and he dressed reasonably well, like he had plenty of money. And he seemed a little awkward. You know, sort of nerdy." She barely took a breath as she continued. "The thing that tipped me off, though, was that he acted kind of cheap when it came to putting stuff together for the so-called romantic dinner. He even asked me if I had a less expensive picnic basket."

Forties. That ruled out the impulsive teens theory.

Donna snorted. "I told him that if he wanted a mass-produced picnic basket, maybe he should go back to the mainland and shop at one of those dollar stores."

"You said his cheapness tipped you off," Abby said. "What did you mean by that?"

Donna looked down at her hands. Then, noticing a price label stuck to the floor, she bent to pick it up. "I don't mean to cast aspersions on anyone's character," she said at last, "but it seemed pretty clear that this tourist was lonely. He was probably desperate for female attention."

"That's odd, then, that he didn't take as much care filling the basket as the young woman did for her parents."

"Exactly. But he was kind of cute in a geeky sort of way, so maybe he thought that was enough to get by on. Who knows, maybe he was having his own version of a midlife crisis."

Abby remembered what Ida had said about her friends relieving the stress of their quarter-life crises by knitting. Things would certainly have turned out differently if this man had chosen to do the same.

"Could you describe him for me?"

The manager thought for a moment, then declared, "He looked a little like Elvis, but with an updated haircut. And, of course, nowhere near as handsome. Pleasant looking, but not anything to write home about."

"So his hair was dark?" Abby ventured.

"Black as a crow's wing. And his eyes had this nice downward slant to them. On a better looking man, my grandmother would have called them 'bedroom eyes.'"

It was a long shot, but Abby decided it was worth a try. "You don't happen to keep the sales receipts back that far, do you?"

"If you're looking for his name and address, I've got nothing. The guy paid cash."

An older couple walked into the store and began browsing. Donna watched to see if they needed her assistance but didn't move from her spot by the coffee mugs. Abby was reminded that afternoon was approaching, so she decided it was time to finish with her questions and move on so she could go back and look for that loggerhead shrike that Conrad claimed to have seen.

"Thank you for your help. Perhaps these clues will help us find one or both of little Moses' parents," Abby said. Unfortunately, none of the information she'd received today had panned out as a direct lead, but perhaps it would help some other piece of the puzzle fall into place.

"Really? Because when Sergeant Cobb was in here the other day, he said it gave him nothing to go on."

CHAPTER ✿ EIGHT

DURING THE WEEK, ABBY had checked in on her parents often, offering to run errands or do whatever else she could to give them a break from caring for Moses. But Ellen had steadfastly insisted that she and George had everything under control. Terza, of course, had been a big help to them, but Joanne Flemming had also come over, bringing foster son Beau with her to see the baby. Even Sam had taken breaks from his farm duties to run errands for George and Ellen.

And then there were the church folks and members of the Senior Center who had taken turns pitching in to bring meals and help with household chores. Terza had acted as the go-to person, using the managerial skills she'd developed while running the family's inn.

"I feel like a real slacker," Abby had said when she called Mary at work Friday afternoon. "I want to do something to help Mom and Dad, but they say everything's already taken care of."

"Henry's working over on Shaw Island tonight, so I'm dateless," Mary replied. "Let's go to the farm after work. I'll cook dinner for Mom and Dad, and you can run the vacuum or scrub a tub or something."

"But they already have a casserole that Emma Stoltz brought over today."

Mary had merely brushed over that. "It'll freeze. Besides, Mom and Dad may not need our food or cleaning, but they need their daughters."

She was right about that. Abby had smiled into the phone. When they were children, her sister had had a tendency to be a bit dictatorial at times, and it had driven Abby crazy. But now that she was older, she had learned to appreciate Mary's take-charge attitude.

And so it happened that they were all seated at the big, round white oak table enjoying what was left of the hamburgers that George had cooked out on the grill, along with Mary's green tomatoes baked in a cornmeal coating, and noodles and summer vegetables tossed with shredded cheese.

Ellen leaned back in her chair, the baby quiet in a homemade sling that hung to her lap. Because she'd been trying to eat without disturbing Moses, the straps of the sling were mottled with tiny splatters of cheese and ketchup. "That was a delicious dinner, Mary. And, Abby, the house looks so tidy. But you two really didn't need to do all of that."

"Yes, we did," Abby said, giving Mary a knowing look.

"Well, I'm glad you came," George said, reaching down to sneak Finnegan a bit of hamburger from his plate. "It's always a treat to see our girls. And Finnegan, too, of course."

Mary didn't say anything about their father's departure

from the no-feeding-from-the-table rule, but Abby was amazed to see that the piece of burger remained where it had dropped. As a well trained service dog, Finnegan knew better than to accept a treat without Mary's permission, so he didn't make a move to touch it. But even though he remained by her chair, with his chin resting on his paws, his eyes repeatedly moved from the burger morsel to Mary.

Abby wiped her mouth then laid her napkin on the table. "Dad, while I was vacuuming I tried to move the bookcase in the front room to clean the baseboards, but it looked like someone has attached the case to the wall."

He straightened, somewhat distracted by Finnegan's refusal to accept the treat. "Yeah, I did that this week. Baby-proofing the house."

"Baby-proofing?" Mary said. "Moses will be gone from here long before he can walk." She cracked a smile at the gung ho way in which their parents had stepped up to the responsibilities of foster parenthood, but it was clear that George and Ellen were dead serious.

Abby rose from the table to clear away some of the dishes. But first she stooped to pick up the forbidden booty from the floor and set it on the counter to give to the dog later. "He's not allowed to have treats until after we've left the table," she reminded their father.

Finnegan heaved a loud sigh and adjusted his chin on his paws.

Ellen picked up where her husband had left off. "Terza said we should secure the bookcase so that if a child climbs up the shelves, it won't fall on him." And before Mary could remind them again that it would be months before Moses would be able to walk or climb, Ellen added, "We thought it would be a good idea so that Emily and Nicholas will be safe when they visit."

Mary's seven- and three-year-old grandchildren were well-behaved, so it would be hard to imagine them climbing on the furniture, but Abby was glad that her parents were taking precautions.

"Yes, that's a good idea," Mary agreed. "Please thank Terza for the suggestion."

Moses squirmed in the sling and Ellen rose from her chair, bracing herself with one hand on the table as she straightened. Then, taking care that Moses was well out of the way of the stove, she put a pan of water on to heat and retrieved a bottle from the refrigerator.

Abby tried to step in and take care of warming the formula for her, but Ellen insisted on doing it herself.

"Mom, aren't you ready for a break? Maybe you should let someone else take over." Abby watched as her mother moved around the kitchen. "It's got to be hard on your back carrying him around like that."

"It rocks him as I move. And, no, it doesn't hurt my back as long as I take plenty of breaks."

"I don't mean a sit-down kind of break," Abby clarified. "What I meant was, maybe it's time to let someone else care for Moses. Someone who's used to taking of children."

She turned to Mary for support.

"Someone a little younger, maybe, who has more energy," Mary added. "You said yourself that there's a long-term foster family on the mainland who's ready to take him in."

The look their mother gave them let them know that that

definitely wasn't an option . . . at least not for now. Once her time was up, Ellen would have no say over where the baby went next, but she had already told Abby about her strong objection to the possibility that Moses would go to live on the mainland.

Ellen carefully turned off the heat and set the bottle in the warm water. "I promised the social worker that I'd care for Moses for the entire two weeks or until the mother is found, whichever is first. And I'm fully prepared to do just that."

"We're worried about you, Mom." Abby continued scraping and rinsing their dinner plates. "And Dad, too. You're both losing sleep."

Ellen moved to stand by George and gently swayed to quiet the baby's complaints of hunger. George reached up and slipped an arm around her waist.

"You don't need to worry about us," she insisted. "We've all slept much better since changing the baby's formula and using the advice that Terza gave us."

A long, uncomfortable silence followed, punctuated only by the intermittent cries from the sling around Ellen's chest. Abby knew that her mother had prayed before taking on this important responsibility and that George fully supported her, but she couldn't help wondering how carefully Ellen was listening for updates on God's plans in this matter.

Ellen lifted the bottle out of the water, shook it, then splashed some on the back of her hand between the thumb and forefinger. Satisfied that the formula was the proper temperature, she returned to her chair and fed Moses.

Abby pulled out her chair and settled onto it. "Why are you doing this, Mom?" Her voice was barely louder than the baby's satisfied grunts. "It's just going to make it harder when you eventually have to give him up. Other foster parents will care for him just as well, even if they are off the island."

But Ellen obviously didn't want to consider that possibility. "It's not that easy. When you find an injured or abandoned baby bird, you care for it yourself, even taking a portable incubator home with you if necessary." She pulled the child closer to her chest as he nursed. "You don't delegate something that important."

Mary and George looked at each other, but neither said a word.

Abby glanced down at her lap for a moment, taking the pause to ask God to guide this conversation in the way that He willed. "I would let someone else do it," she said at last, "if my attachment to the bird prevented it from returning to its flock."

Ellen tensed and it was clear that she didn't like the way this discussion was going. Moses, responding to the unaccustomed stiffness of her embrace, turned away from the bottle.

"I'm sorry, Mom. I wasn't trying to interfere," Abby said.

"Of course not," Mary concurred. "Neither of us is trying to tell you what to do."

Abby met her sister's gaze and gave her a silent *thank you.* "Right. It's just that you seem to be getting very emotionally involved, and we're concerned for you."

While Ellen lifted Moses to pat his back, George leaned forward and rested his forearms on the table. When he spoke, his voice was low and husky.

"Maybe they have a point, honey." He slid a hand across the table to gently touch his wife's arm, but she didn't respond to the contact. "Maybe it has turned personal."

Still holding Moses in the burp position, Ellen wiped the milk from his mouth. Her face instantly became almost crimson and her eyes filled with tears.

"Well, Davy isn't a bird," she said in a strained voice, "and he doesn't have a flock other than me. I *have* to take care of him." Ellen turned her face away and quietly added, "I have to keep him safe."

Mary pushed her wheelchair away from the table and Finnegan lumbered to his feet.

"Davy?"

The word vibrated in the air, echoing through the room just as it echoed through time. Suddenly, things were beginning to make sense and yet not make sense.

George looked frozen as he stared intently at Ellen and deliberated what to do next.

Abby's mind whirled. "Mom?"

With purposeful movements, George rose and walked around the table to stand beside Ellen. His hand rested on her shoulder as she situated Moses back in the sling.

For the first time that Abby could recall, her father looked old. Not chronologically old, the way an eighty-two-year-old man with occasional arthritis looks, but deep-down-in-the-heart old, like someone who has carried a burden for a long time and has grown weary from the effort.

Abby knew her parents well . . . knew that they turned all their cares over to the Lord. But she also knew that some things take a long time to resolve, even with God's help.

"It's getting late," he said, looking at his wristwatch. "Time for us to start getting the little one ready for bed."

He moved from Ellen's side and bent to kiss Mary on the

cheek. His eyes were pink and misty, as if it was all he could do to rein in his long-held emotions.

"Thank you for dinner," he said. "It was delicious." Then a kiss on Abby's cheek. "And thank you for tidying up. We'll talk tomorrow."

Talk, as in chat? Abby thought. *Or really talk about what's going on with Mom and Moses?* Although she was curious for answers, Abby knew that her parents needed to work this out between themselves before discussing it with her and Mary, if at all. One thing she knew for sure: It would all be resolved in God's time.

Abby went around gathering their belongings and promising to stop by and pick up the casserole dish later. As she helped Mary maneuver her wheelchair out the front door, George brought them a small plastic bag.

"Don't forget Finnegan's hamburger."

ALTHOUGH IT HAD RAINED all morning Saturday, the afternoon sunshine had burned away any remaining dampness. The tourists naturally took advantage of what had ultimately turned into beautiful July weather and began congregating in the Green Harbor Park in anticipation of the outdoor concert that was slated to begin at seven o'clock that evening.

Abby and Mary had driven from Little Flock to the park in Mary's van in order to clock the mileage for the walkathon.

Abby set the clipboard down on the console between them. "You can stop here and I'll measure off the bike path."

"Would you mind taking Finnegan with you? He could use some exercise."

"Sure." After Abby lifted the bike down from the back of

the van, she waited while Mary removed the dog's cape and harness and clipped a leash onto his collar. That, along with a word from Mary to tell him to go with Abby, let him know that he was off duty for the next few minutes.

Taking note of the odometer reading on her bicycle, Abby set out with the golden lab to measure the bike path that skirted most of the park's perimeter. Not only had Mary volunteered at the Skills and Crafts leaders' meeting this afternoon to plan the route that the walkathon would take through town, but she'd also enlisted Abby to help her mark the miles and establish appropriate break stations with drinks and snacks for the walkers.

Since most of the route took them from Little Flock along Shoreline Drive and up Kingfisher Avenue, Mary could easily determine the road distance using the van's odometer as she drove. But in order to safely extend the distance to a full ten kilometers without taking the children along roads without sidewalks, they would also make use of the conveniently wide trails around the park.

The going was slow at first as Finnegan stopped occasionally to sniff and explore. But soon the dog was trotting alongside Abby's bike, eager to release some of his pent-up energy.

Abby was glad for the opportunity to release her own pent-up tension as well. The tree-lined path reminded her of a storybook trail with its assorted wildflowers growing among various vines and mosses that covered the ground. It was a peaceful place, even with the sounds of children's laughter and shouts drifting to her as families laid out blankets in the field in front of the temporary stage.

The slight rise of the terrain was giving her a good workout. Judging from the minor exertion on this ride, the trail would be a bit of a push for the children who were in race mode, but taken at a steady walk it could be managed quite comfortably.

As for Mary's wheelchair, the sidewalks should present no problem, but the slope of the trail would definitely pose a challenge. And although the dirt path was well maintained, there were occasional small roots and vines to watch out for. Despite this, Abby knew that her sister was determined enough to overcome the challenge. And if she needed a push or two, well, that's what family and friends were for.

By the time Abby returned to the van, Finnegan's tongue was lolling from his mouth. It was nearing seven o'clock and the temperatures had cooled somewhat, but the humidity lingered in the summer air.

Mary switched off the *Life in Biblical Times* CD she'd been listening to and poured some water in the bowl that she kept in the van for such purposes.

After Abby had loaded the bike and helped Mary put Finnegan's harness and cape back on, Mary drove out of the park and turned right onto Kingfisher Avenue.

"Frank Holloway said he'll provide bottles of water for the walkers in front of his hardware store," Mary said.

Abby nodded. "The park will be another good place to set up a hydration station."

With a sly grin, Mary added, "Brenda Wilson said she'll have ice cream waiting for us when we reach The Tackle Shop since that's nearly the end of the route. Imagine the squeals we'll hear when the kids realize their ice cream came from the same freezer that holds squid for fishing."

Abby laughed, then sat back and watched the First Baptist Church, The Green Grocer, and the Sparrow Island Library pan past Mary's open window. Finally, when she couldn't stand it any longer, she said aloud what both of them had refrained from discussing all day.

"At least now we know what Mom's moods have been about all these years."

The van slowed almost imperceptibly as Mary gave quiet consideration to what Abby had said. "She's a lot more upbeat since Moses came along. Maybe he's what she needed."

"There's no doubt about that. I just worry that she's going to hurt more after Moses leaves than she did before she found him."

From the back of the van, Finnegan strained against his safety strap to push his nose between the seats and lick Abby's elbow. She rubbed the side of the dog's face, laughing as he leaned into it.

"Dad seems to be okay with her keeping Moses for the full two weeks that social services allows for short-term foster parents," Mary said as she made a left onto Primrose Lane.

"He just wants her to be happy."

"That's an understatement if I ever heard one."

"If we want to put a quick end to this, we need to find out who left Moses at the Senior Center," Abby said, knowing that Mary worried when she overstepped her bounds and interfered in Henry's domain. However, they'd both seen the anguish in their mother's eyes when she'd mistakenly called the child by the wrong name. "We need to find that person, for Mom's sake as well as the baby's."

Mary gripped the steering wheel near the top and briefly crossed her thumbs, a sign that she'd just offered up a mini-prayer. "Count me in," she said. "I'll help in whatever way I can."

Just before they reached St. Christopher's Church, Mary pulled into the driveway beside a large, freshly mown lawn that smelled of grass, wild onion and clover.

From behind the attractive Cape Cod house emerged a man in his mid-forties wearing cargo shorts and a baggy T-shirt with the sleeves cut out. He lifted the shirt, baring his belly as he wiped the sweat from his face. Then he pushed his damp hair off his forehead and approached the van wearing a friendly smile that made the craggy complexion of his face seem at once handsome and inviting.

"Hey," he said to Mary as he folded his arms over the lowered van window on the driver's side. "It's too late for you to cut the grass, but you're just in time to help weed the vegetable garden."

"Sorry. A lawn mower and a hoe are too tame for us," Mary said, shaking her head, "but if you've got some fun toys to play with like a backhoe or a bucket loader, then let's talk."

He just chuckled, obviously amused with Mary for taking his bait and tossing it back at him. Abby had to hand it to her sister. She seldom got caught off guard.

"Would you ladies like to come inside?" Vince asked. "Cheryl left a little while ago to go with a friend to the concert in the park, but I'm sure I could rustle up some tea and a few slices of cheesecake."

Abby leaned forward in the passenger seat to remind Mary that they still had more work to do on the walkathon map after they got home, but Mary was already telling Vince that they had only stopped by to measure the remaining distance to his house and see if there was anything else he needed before the walkathon next week.

Since the Emory property was at the end of the ten-kilometer route, he and Cheryl had offered to host a "Post-Pedestrian Pool Party" at their house. Although their children were grown and gone, they were firm supporters of vacation Bible school and all the other children's activities at church.

"No, we're set." He turned to peruse the yard he'd just mown. "I'll just do a quick mow again next week so the kids can play flag football here after their walk. And the pool out back will be ready for them to cool off in. Cheryl's going to take care of the food and I'll just be the general gofer guy."

Mary thanked him profusely and filled him in on approximately how many children and chaperones would attend. Then she turned her attention to other matters. "How are things at the Grace Girls' Home?"

Having formerly worked in the public relations department of a sheet metal company in Bellingham, Vince had recently quit that job to work from home as a fundraiser for various worthwhile charities. The Grace Girls' Home, a temporary shelter for single mothers and mothers-to-be, was particularly close to his heart and he regularly offered his consulting services to them.

Abby knew exactly where Mary was going with her question. Since Henry had surmised that Moses' mother was probably not a teenager from Sparrow Island, Mary was probing to see if perhaps there'd been any recent reports of a runaway.

Vince's face was still red from pushing the lawnmower, and a trickle of sweat escaped from his silver-edged temples and ran down to his jawline where it dangled for a moment before dripping onto his shirt. He pulled a handkerchief from his back pocket and wiped the beads from his forehead and hairline.

"When I heard about the baby that your mother found, Grace Girls was the first place I called. Fortunately, everyone's where they're supposed to be."

Although she was glad to know that all was well at the Grace Girls' Home, Abby's mind was firmly focused on Vince's handkerchief. A white handkerchief with a narrow blue trim, just like the bonnet that had been placed on Moses' head.

She unhooked her seatbelt and leaned toward Mary. "Excuse me. Would you mind telling me where you got that handkerchief?"

Vince stopped shoving the material into his back pocket and pulled it out again to take a look at the sweaty cloth. He shrugged. "I don't know. My wife gave me a package of them for Father's Day last month."

Tempting though it was to go back to the park and find Cheryl to ask her where she'd bought the handkerchiefs, it wasn't very likely they'd find her in the crowd that was milling and dancing to the swing music that was featured tonight.

"Want me to have her call you? We're going to Bellingham to visit her mother tomorrow, but she should be able to give you a call after she gets off work on Monday.

"Thanks, I'd appreciate that," Abby said. "How's she liking her job at The Dorset?"

Vince gave a smile so broad that it was instantly obvious he was proud of his wife. "Loves it," he said. "She's a people person, so working in guest relations lets her talk to people all day long. And since it's only part-time, it's kind of hard for her to overdose on the job."

"Sounds like a perfect match," Abby said.

By now it was a little after seven-thirty. Since they'd spent more time here than anticipated, Mary seemed anxious to say her good-byes and get going.

Vince stood in the yard waving as they left the driveway. After they made a left onto Municipal Street, Mary slowed the van.

"Henry's on duty at the sheriff's station tonight," she said, turning to Abby. "Maybe we should stop in there on the way home and tell him that Cheryl knows where the handkerchief came from."

Enthused by the new lead, Abby told Mary what she'd learned yesterday about the man who had come to Bayside Souvenirs for the picnic basket and beach towel. "Henry had mentioned to the store manager that those sales weren't enough for him to go on, but maybe the handkerchief will produce some possibilities."

As they approached the station, Abby pointed to the sheriff's department car in front of the building. "Isn't that Henry getting out of the car now? And there's someone sitting on the passenger side."

"If he's busy, maybe we shouldn't bother him right now." Mary slowly pulled into the parking area, but she didn't pull up beside his car. Instead, she backed into a parking space at the far·end of the small lot in preparation to turn around and leave.

However, this gave them a perfect view of what was happening in front of the station. Henry looked briefly in their direction as he walked around the car, but he seemed preoccupied with assisting the passenger.

"Yeah, he's busy," Mary said. "I can just tell him when he calls later tonight."

Abby thought it was sweet that Henry made almost nightly check-in calls to Mary. Even though they didn't talk long, it was a nice opportunity to tell each other about their day and say goodnight.

"Wait." Abby laid a hand on Mary's arm. "Who's that getting out of his car?"

They both peered across the parking lot. Although the sun was low in the sky, it was still bright enough to see that the woman he was escorting toward the station had dark, perhaps even black hair. The girl wore a tightly fitted bright pink tank top that left a gap of about three inches of soft fleshy tummy between it and the brown broom skirt that rested low on her hips.

Henry had a hand on the girl's elbow as he guided her toward the front door. When she lifted a hand to her face, he stopped and handed her his handkerchief which she used to wipe her eyes.

Softhearted Mary was instantly sympathetic. "I think she's crying." But just as quickly, her focus took another turn. She put a hand to her heart as she considered a possibility. "I hope she isn't one of those people that Henry sometimes catches bringing drinks into the park."

Abby frowned as she took in the scene. "No, she seems too steady on her feet for that."

Like Mary, Abby was also concerned for the girl, but right now her mind was busy processing the clues they'd gathered so far.

"She's young, maybe college age," Abby observed aloud. "Still of an age to do something as impulsive as leaving her newborn where some senior citizens could find it."

Mary's eyes widened as she realized what Abby was on to. "And look, she's a little thick through the middle."

Mary had always been keen on her own appearance, taking care to stay fairly trim and, of course, well groomed. So it was no surprise that she would notice a trait that could possibly be a sign of a woman who'd recently given birth.

His attitude officious and patient, Henry opened the door for the girl and followed her inside the building.

Mary turned away from the sight and met Abby's gaze. "Are you thinking what I'm thinking?"

Abby gnawed at her bottom lip and gave a quick nod. "If you're thinking this might be the mystery mother, yes, I am."

CHAPTER ❀ NINE

AT CHURCH THE NEXT morning, everyone was buzzing about the woman who'd been taken away from the park in the sheriff's car. Apparently, they'd all come to the same conclusion that Abby and Mary had—that she might be the elusive mother of Moses.

As tempting as it was to try to listen in on the nearest conversation for updates, Abby stayed close to her mother, serving as pack mule for diaper bag and all the other baby paraphernalia as they made their way through the church foyer toward the sanctuary.

Mary was off in the fellowship hall discussing the upcoming walkathon, and George had spotted Rick DeBow and excused himself to ask the handyman's advice on how to repair the Bush Hog attachment for his tractor. That left Abby to remain nearby in case her mother should need a hand with the baby.

Their progress was slow through the foyer as Ellen was stopped multiple times by church members who wanted to take a peek at the baby that slept in the sling around her body.

Each time, Ellen pulled back the fabric strap to show off the baby's straight, dark hair and peacefully sleeping face.

"Oh how nice," Abby said, pointing a stuffed rabbit in the direction of the fellowship hall. "Tamara came back to church, and this time she brought her husband."

Though the couple smiled politely as members welcomed them, Abby noticed an uneasy tension between the pair. They held hands, but it wasn't the comfortable, relaxed kind of turning to each other that happened whenever George and Ellen were together. At first Abby thought it might be because Tamara and Pete were new to the church and were still getting used to it, but they actually seemed more relaxed with the parishioners than they did with each other.

"Tamara? Really?" Ellen turned and looped a hand under the bundle that lay snuggled against her body. "I thought her husband was supposed to leave town again this week for another business trip. I'll be right back," she said and waddled toward the couple.

"Did you hear?" Janet said, coming up beside Abby and grabbing her arm for emphasis.

The church secretary was near bursting to share her scoop. Abby knew that most of her information was dead on target, but there had also been plenty of times when her sources failed her. Janet spotted Mary coming from the fellowship hall and waited for her to join them before continuing.

"Our boys in green arrested Moses' mother at the concert in the park last night. I saw it with my own eyes."

At once, Abby and Mary met each other's gaze. It was just as they had suspected.

Mary's childhood friend had always loved drama and

intrigue. Today she wore a taupe sundress with capped sleeves, and its blandness seemed to make her auburn hair look like a fiery bush on top of her head as she rattled off what she knew.

"Then they whisked her off in a sheriff's department boat over to Friday Harbor so that Judge Swink can decide what to do with her first thing Monday morning."

"Oh dear," Mary said. "It was a foolish thing for her to do, but since the baby wasn't harmed, I hope they'll go easy on her."

"Even if she wants to keep Moses and they cut her some slack, she probably won't get him back right away," Janet said in a manner that indicated she knew more about these things than she really did. "They'll probably take him out of short-term foster care soon and place him elsewhere while they decide what to do next."

Janet raised a good point. Abby wondered if the mother would eventually be reunited with her son. Or if she even wanted him at all. The letter she'd left in the basket indicated that she did, indeed, love him and that her actions had been motivated by a lack of a proper environment in which to raise the boy.

Abby sighed with frustration as she recalled Henry's recent update that the analysis of the letter was mostly fruitless. Although the paper and ink had been generic office items just as he had expected, the sheriff had mentioned something about a small distinction in the block lettering. Unfortunately, it wasn't enough to lead them to any particular letter writer.

"We should pray for the mother," Abby said, hoisting the diaper bag up on her shoulder. "And especially for Moses."

The three women held hands and silently turned over their concerns to the Lord.

"Amen," the three said after a quiet moment. Janet looked past Abby and Mary toward her office and an expression of mild alarm crossed her face. "I hate to rush off, but it looks like Rev. Hale's looking for his sermon notes. If I don't help him find them now, both our offices will be torn to smithereens in a matter of minutes."

As they watched her go, the weight of the prayer still heavy on their hearts and their hands still joined, Mary turned to Abby.

"Well, it looks like we won't need to track down that handkerchief after all."

AFTER THEY'D SETTLED into their usual seats at the back of the church and waited for Rev. Hale to take his place at the lectern, Abby tried to clear her mind so she'd be receptive to the sermon.

Ellen placed a hand on her knee and leaned close. "Pray for Tamara and Pete," she said, nodding toward the couple who sat across the aisle from them. "They're having a bumpy time of it lately."

Speaking quietly as the opening music played, Abby turned to her mother. "Of course I'll pray for them." In fact, she'd started last week after meeting the sad-faced young woman who'd looked so ill in the heat. Abby had worried that the unseasonable temperature might keep her from coming back, but apparently Tamara had liked Little Flock well enough to give it another try. "It's nice that her husband can be with her today." Abby paused and put a finger to her chin. "But I thought that he was only supposed to be home for a day or two during the week, and then head out for another business trip."

"That was the plan. Two days home, and then another two weeks away," Ellen said. "But I guess whatever's going on between them was enough to cause him to cancel." She pressed her lips together and rubbed the bundle on her lap as she considered the couple's trouble. "Apparently, he's not very happy about having to change his plans."

Glancing over at the couple, Abby noticed Tamara looking over her shoulder toward them. Her husband sat stiffly beside her, as if he was anxious for the service to be over so he could leave.

There was plenty of room in the Stanton's pew for the couple to join them. It was odd that they'd chosen to sit on the opposite side of the church with strangers instead of with people they knew.

Abby smiled back at her, but either Tamara didn't see her or she was so caught up in her own thoughts that she didn't respond. She was such a pretty young woman—blue eyes, delicate porcelain skin and pale blonde hair—but she seemed so very sad. *It must be incredibly lonely for a woman when her husband was away more than he was at home.* And Ellen had indicated that Tamara's shyness kept her even further isolated.

In that case, it was a good thing that she had chosen to start attending Little Flock. Everyone needed a good church family. If Tamara and her husband attended regularly, it wouldn't be long before they'd feel like they were coming home to a weekly family reunion with spiritual brothers and sisters, aunts and uncles, nieces and nephews.

On the row in front of the Prestons, Jenny and her husband Steve sat with their former houseguest, Charlotte. Although

Jenny was in the middle, an uncomfortable distance remained between her and Charlotte. Abby sighed, distressed that two long-time friends would let a baby—one to which neither of them had any claim—come between them.

The deacon stepped to the podium and led the congregation in an opening prayer. Abby took that time to offer up special prayers for Tamara, Pete, Jenny and Charlotte, as well as the dark-haired woman who'd been taken into custody last night.

Then came the announcements. Rev. Hale took the podium, making special note of the Skills and Crafts group's upcoming walkathon and urging members to sponsor a walker. As the preacher spoke, Bobby triumphantly flipped through the pages of signatures on his sponsor list. Sandy McDonald quietly placed a hand over her son's fidgeting fingers. Chastised, the boy tucked the sheets on the bench beside him and settled into a posture of polite attentiveness.

Rev. Hale continued on to the prayer requests, asking for prayers for various shut-ins and for those who were sick or away on vacation. For a second, Abby smiled to think of resident islanders going to the mainland for their vacations, when so many people from all over North America and even around the world flocked to the San Juan Islands for their own getaways.

"I'd also like for you to open your hearts to a young woman who has recently encountered some trouble in her life," said the pastor as he paced in front of the group. "One moment she was sitting in the park, waiting for a friend to join her for an evening of music, and the next she was being approached by an officer from the sheriff's department with some devastating news."

Abby turned to Mary on her right. Mary reached over and took her hand, clasping their fingers together. Abby squeezed back.

The congregation had grown silent. Not so much as a shoe scraping the floor broke the silence as they waited for further information about this morning's main topic of discussion.

"Her family's house had been destroyed by fire," he continued, "and a family member had to be taken to the hospital, but it wasn't certain whether that family member would make it through the night."

Heads turned and whispers rippled through the pews as folks tried to match this up with what they'd heard this morning about the woman in the park. Ellen wrapped her hands around the little bundle on her lap, and George slipped his arms around his wife's shoulders.

Rev. Hale spoke over the hum of whispered conversations. "As is typical of the caring service provided by our sheriff's department officials for locals and tourists alike, Sergeant Cobb took the call after family members were unable to reach her cell phone. After locating the woman at the park, he took her to the sheriff's station."

By now the buzz had died down as everyone strained to hear every word he said.

"And so that this young woman in need wouldn't be delayed three hours waiting for the next ferry, Sergeant Cobb personally took her in a sheriff's department boat to the mainland so she could return to her family as quickly as possible."

Mary leaned in and whispered, "That must be why Henry didn't call last night to tell me goodnight."

"And why he's not here this morning," Abby said, thinking

of the long boat trip he had made. "He must have slept in after getting home so late."

"God is good," Rev. Hale continued. "Although the family lost all of their personal belongings in the fire, everyone's safe." He grinned as he added the next part. "It turns out the 'family member' that was taken to the hospital was a cat, but I'm told it's going to be just fine after it recovers from a bit of smoke inhalation."

Ellen raised her hand to speak, and the pastor nodded at her.

"The people of Sparrow Island have been extremely kind about making blankets and sweaters and booties for little Moses," she said. "In fact, we have so many nice things for the baby that he'll never be able to use them all." She paused and patted the boy's diapered bottom. "Perhaps those who know how to knit and quilt could put those skills to work making blankets for this family that has been so hard hit."

Heads nodded throughout the church, and a couple of ladies offered to donate embroidered sheet sets. Then Thelma Rogers rose to her feet. She could be rather curmudgeonly at times, speaking out occasionally against certain proposed church activities, so Abby wondered if she was going to protest this spontaneous plan.

Instead, she shocked them all by suggesting that the church collect a special offering for the family. "Even if they have fire insurance, it could be a while before the check comes," Thelma said. "So a gift certificate from a discount department store will allow them to buy some of the things they need right away."

All agreed it was an excellent idea, and the offering plate was passed.

A warm feeling came over Abby as she placed a check in the plate. It felt good to be able to respond quickly when someone needed their help. It also felt good that her mother had started Thelma and the church thinking in a way that had led to this gift.

However, although the identity of the woman Henry had escorted into the sheriff's station last night was resolved, they still didn't know the identity of the woman who'd given birth to Moses.

ALTHOUGH HENRY HADN'T MADE IT to church after his late night, he had made plans to meet the family for lunch at the Stanton Farm afterward. Abby wanted to make their way through the crowd to get to the farm as quickly as possible so she could fill Henry in on the clue she'd uncovered about Vince's handkerchief and find out what else the sheriff might have learned in the past few days.

However, the others didn't seem to notice her eagerness to leave. Mary and George were off talking to Martin and Terza, and Jenny and Charlotte had swarmed to Ellen like bees to honey.

Abby made small talk with Joanne and Clint Flemming while Charlotte gushed loudly over the baby. Although it wasn't overt, Abby was aware of the way Charlotte had shouldered her way between the baby and Jenny. Despite the snub, Jenny waited patiently for her turn to peek at the baby.

While his foster parents talked with Abby, Beau climbed up onto a nearby pew and craned his head to see what the other women were exclaiming about. His speech, though difficult to understand because of the cleft palate, was clear enough for them to know that he wanted to see the baby who Charlotte was making such a fuss over.

Jenny moved around behind her friend and picked the toddler up. "Beau wants to see too," she said, sidling in closer.

Not a shy child at all, Beau leaned forward and patted Charlotte on the arm. "*Um shee*," he said as best he could.

Charlotte drew back at his touch and stared at the child for a long moment. "What's wrong with him?"

Jenny gave her friend a scowl and a sharp nudge with her elbow, then asked Beau the color of the baby's sleeper. When he said something that sounded like "*Ghoo*," she excitedly affirmed him. "That's right, it's blue!"

By this time, Abby and the Flemmings ceased their conversation. Beau was focused solely on the baby that Ellen had taken out of the sling to show everyone, and he seemed not to have heard what had been said about him. But Joanne had heard.

She squared her shoulders and spoke softly but firmly. "Not a thing," she said, answering Charlotte's insensitive question. "He's absolutely perfect."

A long, strained silence stretched out between them. Abby didn't bother to smooth it over, knowing that Charlotte needed to realize how unkind her question had sounded. However, the woman merely lifted a shoulder and turned her attention back to Moses, claiming that the baby looked like her and thus was the reason she should be the one to have him.

Bobby bounded past them, playfully grabbing Beau by the nape of the neck as he passed and causing the child to squeal with delight. Then he went over to Mary, probably to clear up some details about the walkathon.

But although the moment had passed and Charlotte seemed oblivious to the potential hurtfulness of her words, Jenny clearly was having trouble dealing with her friend's attitude.

Still holding the toddler on her hip, and giving him a little hug, she said to Abby, "I don't know if I'm going to feel like coming for the rest of the bird-watching outings this week."

She didn't have to say why. Everyone knew. Including Charlotte, who rolled her eyes.

"If you want me to go home, just say so, but don't expect me to back down from trying to adopt Moses. I've already talked to Randy about it, and he agrees we should have him."

From her tone, Abby got the impression that Charlotte's husband didn't dare disagree with anything she had set her mind to do.

But Charlotte's marriage was the least of Abby's concerns right now. Although any birder was free to drop out of the bird-watching hikes at any time during the course, she was concerned that if either of the friends did so, it would widen the rift that had grown between them.

Bored with the baby and their discussion, Beau leaned toward Clint who hefted him onto his hip.

Jenny bristled in response to her friend's comment. "I was just saying that you might enjoy it better if I wasn't there."

Abby moved closer to Jenny and laid a hand on her back. "Please don't let this get in the way of your friendship," she said to both women. "It's not worth it. I know this from personal experience."

Charlotte lifted her chin. "You don't know what it's like to have someone criticizing your choices all the time and trying to tell you what to do."

Ellen threw a cloth over her shoulder and lifted Moses to rub his back in small circles. He'd finished a bottle just before the service ended, and now he was restless. However, Ellen's attention was focused squarely on the drama that was unfolding between these two friends.

"What I *do* know is that my sister Mary and I were separated for a lot of years, not only in miles but in our hearts." Her hand still on Jenny as she tried to underscore the sincerity of her words, Abby leaned past her to make eye contact with Charlotte. "Don't waste years that you can't get back."

Beau flung himself forward in Clint's arms, trying to get Joanne's attention. She held out her hands to take him, but he refused, trying to tell her something that none of them understood.

"Speak slowly so I can hear you," his foster mother said patiently. "Take your time."

He tried again, but once again it sounded garbled. Finally, frustrated, the child pointed to Moses and yelled, "Mama, yook!"

That everyone understood. They all turned toward the baby in time to see a dribble of milk burble over from the baby's mouth onto the spit-up cloth. But the tummy overflow was minor compared to Joanne's look of surprise over having been called Mama.

Quickly, she regained her composure and calmly said, "I'm Joanne, sweetie." Then she reached over and wiped up the drip with a clean tissue that she pulled from her pocket.

Clint shifted the boy in his arms. "We'll meet you at the car," he said.

When Beau was safely out of earshot, Joanne said, "He's

been with us so long that he's thinking of me as his mother." She sighed with a hint of dismay, as if she had been anticipating this day. "He needs a permanent home before he becomes too firmly bonded to Clint and me."

Abby's gaze went to the tiny baby in her mother's arms.

That made two.

CHAPTER ✿ TEN

Neither Jenny nor Charlotte came birding with the group on Monday morning. After their display of testiness at church yesterday, Abby had hoped they would settle their differences and focus on more important things such as their longtime friendship. Since they'd already paid for the ten-day class, their absence shouldn't bother Abby, but it did. For one, this was the first such class offered by the conservatory and she wanted it to be a success, complete with word-of-mouth recommendations. But the main reason was that she hated to see a friendship fall apart over something that could be worked out with a little honest communication.

As for the competing cousins, Warren and Conrad were still up to their one-upmanship antics. Though they were both in their forties, they'd acted like a couple of schoolboys horsing around and shoving each other until Abby reminded them that the birds they'd come to see wouldn't linger nearby if they kept at it.

"All right, guys, cut it out," Tom said when the pair made one more attempt to snatch each other's birding journals.

Though his words were spoken softly, they held a firmness that was backed up by his sheer size. At six feet, four inches and at least 250 pounds, he was a man not easily ignored.

Embarrassed to have been called down for the second time, this time more sternly, Conrad and Warren sheepishly set about the task of launching their rented johnboat into Cedar Grove Lake.

Abby climbed into the three-person boat with the cousins, resolving to use the "teacher glare" she'd honed at Cornell University should the two men decide to continue their rowdy horseplay.

As they paddled quietly along the edge of the freshwater lake, Abby let the serenity of her surroundings and the rhythmic movement of the oars release the tension from her neck and shoulders. Along the shore, crickets and toads competed to fill the air with their sounds. It was an outdoor concert of divine proportions.

The trio of boats moved smoothly near the shore, their aluminum sides occasionally swishing past the thick stands of marsh grass. With a finger raised to her lips, Abby turned and pointed toward a shimmering movement in the shallow water. The two yellowish strips running along its body identified the water snake as a common garter. To her amusement, the only one who reacted with alarm was Tom, the man who was built like he'd once played a defensive position in football. Leaning to the far side of the boat—the side *away* from the snake—he paddled furiously to put more distance between himself and the serpent.

When they passed a wooden post beheaded of the nest box that had once sat there, Abby explained to the group that it had originally been placed too far into the open and was later moved under the shelter of overhanging trees. The kindhearted person who had put it there had meant well, but obviously hadn't researched to learn the best locations for wood duck nest boxes.

"What's wrong with this spot?" Shelley asked. "When the baby ducks are ready to leave the nest, they could jump directly from the box into the water."

"True," Abby said, "but in this case the nest was so obvious to other hens looking for a place to lay their eggs that they didn't bother searching elsewhere, even though this one had already been taken. So as soon as one hen had lain her eggs and left the nest, another one came in and laid hers on top of them. The process continued until the box was full of eggs, most of which never hatched." She paused, remembering the sulfurous odor of rotten eggs when she'd examined the box after breeding season was over. "In this case, nearly thirty eggs were dumped, but only the top three or four hatched. Most of the time when it gets that bad, all of the hens just abandon the nest box."

A few more strokes of the oars took the birders to the shade of the maple, birch and fir trees that bordered the lake. Once their eyes adjusted to the dimmer light, Abby pointed out several nest boxes that had been installed after the other had been taken down. These were harder not only for predators to find, but also for competing ducks intent on claiming squatter's rights.

A pair of pileated woodpeckers swung past, and as quickly as they had appeared, they disappeared behind a stout tree trunk, and soon their resonating pecks could be heard echoing over the water.

Some birders considered the summer months to be a "dead" time for bird-watching. Sure, some of the creatures were less visible since their courtship rituals and nesting were mostly over by now, but Abby considered any time of the year prime for observing her feathered friends. The quickly filling journals of her fellow enthusiasts was evidence of that.

"Most of the nest boxes are probably empty by now," Abby continued, "but there may be a few overachievers working on their second or even third broods at this time of year. In the fall, volunteers from the conservatory will come out and check the condition of the boxes and discard any dumped eggs in preparation for next year's breeding season. Then the boxes will probably be used by screech owls and other birds as a warm roost for the winter."

The group moved on, their focus shifting to other birds as they floated past. Although Abby was going through the motions of describing various birds and their peculiar habits, her thoughts kept returning to the friends who were competing to adopt Moses.

As with wood ducks, some healthy competition was a good thing. By striving for food, mates and nesting space, the birds strengthened their bodies and sharpened their skills. This, of course, was according to God's perfect plan. However, when competition became unhealthy, with the ducks all vying for the same nest box, the results could be . . . well, rather stinky.

Unfortunately, that's exactly what Charlotte and Jenny were doing . . . competing for the same nesting opportunity. Abby prayed they would see that Moses wasn't their only option for a family, preferably before their friendship died like those dumped eggs.

ON HER WAY BACK to the conservatory from The Bird Nest where most of the birders were staying, Abby drove east on Shoreline Drive, took a left on Primrose Lane and immediately doglegged into the parking lot at The Dorset. Vince had said he would have Cheryl call after her work-shift today, but Abby found herself feeling a little too antsy to wait for the phone to ring.

After locking the van, she strolled past the fountain and stone bench at the front of the elegant building toward the brass front doors attended by a uniformed doorman. The weather had been perfect this morning, and Abby found herself wishing she had time to make use of the brick labyrinth in the hotel courtyard for a walking meditation.

But first things first. As she entered the plush lobby, she was once again overwhelmed with the elegance of the place. At the registration desk, Cheryl Emory looked quite official in her crested jacket and brass nametag as she finished checking out a sunburned guest. A skinny young fellow in a similar outfit offered to assist Abby, but she smiled and indicated that she would wait for Cheryl.

Perched on the circular couch, Abby discreetly studied the man checking out of the hotel. Remembering what Donna Morgan had said about the probable father of Moses looking like Elvis with an updated haircut, she noted the dark hair, square-cut jaw and slim good looks. This guy also looked to be about forty years old, but he moved with an easy confidence that told her this probably wasn't the same guy. Still, she wanted him to turn around so she could check to see if he had "bedroom eyes."

Oh come on, Abby, she chided herself. *Why would that guy be anywhere near Sparrow Island now? After all, he was on vacation nine months ago.* Obviously, her radar was on hyper-alert today.

Even so, she watched as the man gathered his belongings to leave and dragged his suitcase behind him. When he turned and gave her a shy smile, she realized she must have been staring harder than she'd intended.

Hoping she hadn't embarrassed him with her bold attention, she waited until he'd left the lobby before rising from the sofa, then walked over to the registration desk where Cheryl was finishing up his checkout paperwork.

"I love attending to first-time guests at The Dorset," Cheryl said. "They're always so excited about the luxury and elegance of the place. The guy who just left was here on business, but he liked it so much that he booked a suite for him and his wife to celebrate their fifteenth anniversary in a couple of months."

Just as she had thought. A coincidence. But it wouldn't hurt to double check. "How do you know it was his first visit?"

"Other than his excitement over being here? We have a database of all our guests and I had to input his information." Cheryl placed the signed receipt in a wire basket with several others. "He just moved to Oregon from Richmond, England. Did you hear his accent? It made me have a flashback to the Beatles."

Okay, definitely a coincidence. If the man Donna had sold the basket to had spoken with a British accent, she most certainly would have mentioned it.

Having bypassed the usual pleasantries, Abby suddenly remembered her manners. "I hope you enjoyed your visit with your mother yesterday."

"Thank you. It's always good to see her. Hey, I was going to call you later today," Cheryl said, clicking out of the computer.

"Vince said you and Mary wanted to buy some handkerchiefs like his for your dad."

Actually, that wasn't what they'd said, but now that she mentioned it, it sounded like a pretty good idea.

"The handkerchiefs are so distinctive," Abby replied. "We were curious to know where you'd found them."

Cheryl smiled and asked the other clerk to cover for her momentarily. Then, stepping out from behind the desk, she motioned Abby to follow her.

"How are things going with baby Moses?" Cheryl asked as she guided them past the elevator.

"He's doing great. Mom says the little rascal loves to eat."

"Still no sign of the parents?"

Abby shook her head and summarized the conversation she'd had with Henry at lunch yesterday.

"The sheriff's department is 'still working on it.'" She hooked her fingers to add air quotes, indicating this had come directly from Henry.

She didn't bother to mention that Henry didn't seem very interested in the connection she and Mary had made with the handkerchief. He had merely thanked them for the information and indicated that he and his deputies might be on to something more substantial. No matter how close his relationship was with Mary and the rest of the Stantons, Sergeant Henry Cobb was professional to the core. Confidential information stayed confidential as far as he was concerned.

Cheryl stopped at the hotel gift shop, opened the door and followed Abby in. She crossed the room, bypassing the shelf of pain relievers, toothpaste and breath mints, and stopped at a three-tiered plant stand that held not plants but small gift packages with samples of what was inside laid out beside the cream colored boxes tied with burgundy ribbons. One tier held ladies' scarves, another small sailboat tie pins, and the bottom one held both men's and women's handkerchiefs.

"They're rather pricey," Cheryl said apologetically as she handed the sample to Abby, "which is why I was glad to have an employee discount when I bought them for Vince's Father's Day gift."

Abby caught a glimpse of the price tag and decided that the discount was a good thing, especially considering that Vince had used his gift as a sweat mop while mowing. She examined the elegant linen handkerchief and the narrow blue stitching around the edge. Since she had memorized the pictures she'd taken of Moses and the items he'd been found with, it wasn't necessary to retrieve the camera for comparison. This was exactly like the bonnet that had been carefully placed on the baby's head before he was left at the Senior Center.

A tiny woman who appeared to be of mixed East Indian heritage stepped out from behind the counter and joined them. Although she wore slacks and a top, the rich gold and ivory fabric of her blouse gave the impression of a sari. Her name badge read *Sarika*.

"That's fine Irish linen," the woman said. "You won't find handkerchiefs like those anywhere else."

Abby turned it over in her hand, examining the intricately detailed stitching and hoping that the piece would somehow impart some information—or maybe even a hint—to her.

"What makes those handkerchiefs so special is that we have master artisans on the islands who do the embroidery."

Abby's thoughts drifted back to Sunday, a week ago, when

so many people at church had pulled out their handkerchiefs to wipe their foreheads when the temperatures had soared outside. Other than the ladies' hankies, she didn't recall seeing any men's cloths with this type of blue edging.

Of course, this was the kind of thing that a vacationer to the island would buy—a functional souvenir. When locals came to The Dorset, it was to be pampered at the day spa, attend a wedding in the luxurious ballroom or hold meetings in the hotel's elegantly furnished mahogany library. It didn't seem likely that local residents would pop into the gift shop to buy an expensive souvenir.

Abby looked up from the handkerchief to the woman who had given her the information and was taken aback by her features. Ordinarily, she would have been bowled over by the extraordinary beauty of the diminutive woman, but today all she noticed was the sleek dark hair that fell to the middle of her back and the deep brown, almond-shaped eyes that grew quizzical under Abby's intense gaze.

Just like Moses Doe's.

A fleeting second after the thought crossed her mind, Abby realized that, once again, her imagination was running away with her. Until Moses' parents were found, it seemed that every dark-haired, brown-eyed person who crossed her path was destined to trigger the *what if?* response in Abby's mind.

As far as this "suspect" went, a second glance showed that she wasn't nearly as young as Abby had originally supposed. A few threads of silver at her temples hinted at the need for a touch-up, and fine smile lines around those beautiful brown eyes suggested that she was closer in age to Abby than to the girl in the park that Henry had helped Saturday night.

And even if she had been of childbearing age, her petite size would have clearly revealed to those around her the changes taking place in her body.

"Would you like to buy it?" Sarika asked. "They come two to a box."

"*Um*, I don't—" Even as she spoke, Abby thought of her father who had been so devoted in helping her mother care for the baby this past week. A nice handkerchief like this would look good peeking out of the breast pocket of his blue suit. "Yes, thank you. I'd like this for my father."

The woman smiled and slipped the pre-wrapped box into a bag marked with a cursive *D* for Dorset.

After Abby paid for the handkerchiefs, Cheryl walked with her back to the lobby. It was then that Abby revealed her belief that the baby's father may have stayed at The Dorset last fall. She was convinced that the handkerchief came from the same person who had bought the picnic basket and beach towel.

It was a long shot, but she had to ask. "You mentioned that the hotel keeps a database of its customers. Is there any chance you could look someone up for me?"

Cheryl straightened the lapel of her burgundy blazer. "I'm sorry, but we're under strict orders to protect the privacy of our patrons."

"Of course," Abby agreed. "I understand."

She thanked Cheryl for her help and drove the van back to the conservatory.

On the way, she considered how a lonely man looking for companionship—as Donna had described him a rich, good looking man with dark hair and bedroom eyes—might have come to Sparrow Island during the busy tourist time of the Flashback Festival and decided to use the opportunity for his own selfish purposes.

He must have been traveling in style, given that he had probably stayed at The Dorset, where he bought a handkerchief from the gift shop.

But Donna had said that this fellow had planned to have a romantic picnic in front of a fireplace. To her knowledge, though, there were no fireplaces in any of the private rooms at The Dorset. Just one in the lobby and another in the ballroom upstairs.

So if the couple didn't have their rendezvous at The Dorset, then he must have gone to her place.

But where was her place? One of the smaller hotels or bed-and-breakfast inns on the island? Although Abby had grown up on Sparrow Island, she hadn't been in all of these places. Then again, if the mother was a local girl, perhaps he had gone to her house.

First things first. The Chois would know which, if any, of the rooms for rent on the island featured fireplaces. When Martin and Terza had restored the turn-of-the-century Victorian house to its original finery a number of years ago, they had inspected the other B&Bs for ideas on how to update the place while still giving it a feel of historic authenticity.

Yes, they would know whether there were rooms for rent with fireplaces. Tomorrow morning, when she drove to The Bird Nest to pick up the birders, she would ask the Chois.

Tomorrow.

If her curiosity would let her wait that long.

CHAPTER ✾ ELEVEN

ELLEN HAD JUST PUT THE baby down in his bassinet when the car pulled into the Stanton's long driveway.

Perfect timing.

She opened the door and greeted Terza with a hug. Raising a finger to her lips, she led her friend toward the coffee table where she had prepared tea. She'd been looking forward to this visit all morning.

"I'm hoping Moses will sleep while we visit," Ellen said.

On the way through the front room, Terza paused in front of the bookcase and gave it a little tug. "George did a nice job. It's very secure."

"We're glad to keep our great grandchildren and any other little visitors safe while they're here." Ellen motioned toward the comfortable chair—the one that matched hers and in which George usually sat—for Terza to sit while she finished with the tea. "How's your finger?"

Terza held out her index finger. Only a pink line remained where the cut had been. "Much better. I put honey on it at night to kill the germs, and aloe in the mornings to help it heal faster."

A plate of cookies, covered in festive blue plastic wrap and tied with a silver ribbon, sat on the table.

"Help yourself," Ellen said as she poured hot water into a cup and set it and a dessert plate before her friend. "The divinity is from the preacher's wife, and Janet made her famous seven-layer bars."

A muffled squeak came from the direction of the bassinet, so Ellen leaned over the upholstered arm of her chair to peek into the basket without actually getting up. Moses had managed to free one tiny fist from the blanket, and now he swung it in the air. All looked well, so she decided to let him stay there in hopes that he'd settle down and go back to sleep.

"Honestly, that is the hungriest little baby I've ever seen," she told Terza. "I think he must have smelled the spice tea and got all stirred up."

Her guest smiled proudly. "If he likes tea, he must take after his honorary Aunt Terza."

"Oh, before I forget," Ellen said, helping herself to a cup of the steaming liquid, "Abby called and wants me to ask you whether any of the inns or hotels on the island have fireplaces in the guest rooms. Would you mind giving her a call when you get a chance?"

"Sure, but I don't know of any places like that. Most of the inns around here have a fireplace in a common area of the house."

Before long, the two women were talking about everything from the lavender that George grew on the farm to funny stories about previous guests who had stayed at The Bird Nest. It was hard to believe Terza was a year younger than her own daughter's fifty-five years. But Ellen had learned long ago that chronological age was less important than what one did with his or her time. And she was glad to have friends who used their years well for the Lord.

As Ellen gazed across the room at the sweet, funny and strong little woman who had become such a big part of her life this past week, she silently thanked God for having given her the opportunity to build a closer relationship with Terza.

She set her tea cup on the end table. "You know, it's amazing that during the ten or so years you've lived here in Green Harbor, this is the most time we've ever spent together." Ellen leaned back in her chair and put her feet up on the ottoman for a much-earned rest. "I admit to feeling a little guilty for pulling you away from your work, but I'm so glad Moses gave us this chance to get to know each other better."

Terza smiled, her teeth seeming even whiter in contrast to the red lipstick that she'd worn for the occasion. "This is like a vacation for me," she said. "Martin says I deserve time off because I've been working so hard, so he hired Eileen Minsky to give us a hand with some of the household tasks."

"Ah, yes. For a teenager, she's a regular worker bee. Takes after her dad. She used to cut our grass for us whenever George and Sam didn't have the time."

"Martin's getting help with the outside work too." Terza chuckled and covered her mouth with her hand. As she spoke, her Chinese accent became more pronounced, which was something that happened anytime her emotions were heightened. And right now she was struggling to hold back a case of the giggles. "Two of our male guests have helped him with the yard work—trimming bushes and painting the trim on the house."

"How sweet!" Ellen exclaimed. "Here these people are on their vacation, yet they're laboring in the yard of The Bird Nest."

"And we're very grateful. But here's the funny part." Terza shook her head, sending her black pageboy-cut hair bouncing against her cheek. "They turned it into a contest. Two grown men trying to see who could cut more bushes in the least time. We've never seen two people work so fast. Or so many bushes trimmed in so little time."

"A contest? I wonder if these are the same men that Abby says have turned bird-watching into a competitive sport."

"Yes, same people. They make me think of little boys, each trying so hard to do better than the other."

She giggled again, and this time Moses joined in with some squawking and squirming of his own.

"Speaking of little boys . . ." Ellen rose to attend to him, but Terza jumped up and waggled her hand at her to stay right where she was.

"Auntie Terza will get him." She carefully lifted the child out of the bassinet and kissed him on his black hair. The crying instantly stopped. Then she held him in front of her and stared at his face. "Look at those eyes."

She lifted the baby up to her face and beamed broadly, her cheek touching his. Moses blinked and turned toward her, his tiny mouth open.

"See? He's Chinese, like me."

"Wait. Don't move." Ellen scrambled out of the chair and retrieved the camera from the hall table where George had left it. "This is one for the scrapbook."

The two women laughed while they took turns mugging for the camera. For one of them, Ellen held the baby between them, and Terza's arm looped around her shoulders while squeezing off a frame with the camera in her other hand.

"I hate to break it to you," Ellen said at last, between fits of laughter, "but Dr. Randolph says your honorary nephew is as white as I am."

Terza's smile never wavered. "That's okay. I'll declare my honorary nephew an honorary Asian." Hugging the baby to her chest, she sat back down and cuddled him.

Ellen watched, thinking how much joy such a tiny little person could bring into people's lives. Terza started out making nonsense baby-talk, then drifted into her native tongue, her voice full of happy energy. For a moment, it seemed as though Terza had forgotten there was anyone in the room besides her and Moses.

There were moments when Ellen felt that way too. Holding Moses and spending time with him had a way of making her remember the good times and forget the other part. Ellen had faith in God, and He had helped her get back on her spiritual feet since that time so many years ago. But still . . . the time she spent with baby Moses was a gift. And Ellen wanted to make the most of this gift that she possibly could.

After a moment, Terza grew silent. The baby lay on her lap, looking up at her. Her gaze didn't leave his face, but it was apparent that her thoughts had taken her far away.

"I have nephews and nieces in Hong Kong," she said at last. "They are grown now and some have children of their own. Martin and I go back to see them whenever we can."

She grasped the baby's hands, his fingers closing around her thumbs, and she moved his arms around in a motion that resembled a fluid, slow-motion dance. Moses, happy for the attention, lay there trying to focus on Terza's face.

Ellen still had the camera in her hand, but to take a picture now would interrupt the quiet connection that was taking place between her friend and the baby. She set the camera down on the end table beside her and waited. She could tell there was something more that Terza had to say, but she didn't want to probe. Terza would talk when she was ready. And if she wasn't ready today, she might be ready tomorrow. Or a month from now or a year from now. Ellen knew from her own experience that there were certain discussions that shouldn't be rushed.

Terza toyed with the baby's miniature fingers, then her gaze settled on the healing mark along her own finger.

"You and George must have thought I was crazy when I came in here and started baby-proofing the place," she said at last.

With a shake of her head, Ellen let her eyes drift to the piano, wishing life was as black and white as the keys on the instrument. "No," she said. "I assumed you had a good reason."

"I did have a good reason." Terza waited another long moment, this one stretching out until Ellen assumed that was all she was going to say about the matter.

When the room was so quiet that even Moses didn't stir, Ellen was about to change the subject to something that wasn't quite so emotionally charged. Patricia Hale's divinity cookies, perhaps.

Terza bowed her head. Ellen wasn't sure whether she was offering a gesture of respect, gazing at the baby or perhaps praying. After a moment, Terza cleared her throat.

"His name was Zhi Ming."

ABBY SAT AT HER DESK, staring blindly at the quarterly report that needed to be filled in with sightings of birds during their outings. The deadline for the next one was a couple of months away, but Abby liked to update her own records every week. In this case, she was wondering whether she should take a chance and notify the birding authorities of this latest unusual sighting or follow her hunch and dismiss it as a bunch of malarkey.

First, there was Conrad's loggerhead shrike. Now his cousin Warren was claiming to have spotted a red-legged kittiwake, and Conrad confirmed it. The black-legged variety was considered to be very rare in the San Juan Islands, but the red-legged bird had never been officially seen nor did it have appropriate documentation. Another such sighting, even if it was classified as hypothetical, could stir undue interest among the birding community, especially if, as Abby suspected, the cousins were mistaken about what they'd seen.

A Sabine's gull, also very rare in these parts but more likely to be seen than the red-legged kittiwake, was close enough in appearance to be mistaken for the other bird if seen only at a glance. However, the Sabine's gull's dark gray hood should have differentiated it from the kittiwake's plain white head and neck. But both cousins had sworn they'd seen it, and Warren was especially vociferous about claiming to have been the first to have spied the bird.

She'd had other amateur birdwatchers make mistakes, but over the past week she'd come to see that these two guys really knew their birds. And that was why she hadn't just summarily dismissed their claims.

Abby ran her hands through her chin-length brown hair, and when her fingers reached the ends she gave a frustrated little pull. She absolutely loved this job, but sometimes it made her want to yank out her hair.

The phone rang and she scooped up the receiver before the first tone ended. "Abby Stanton, Sparrow Island Nature Conservatory."

"Oh good, you're at your desk. I was afraid you'd be out in the field somewhere."

"Cheryl?"

"Yes. I only have a minute, but after we spoke this morning, my fingers did a little walking through the computer database."

Abby picked up a pencil and poised it over a pad of paper. "Go ahead."

"Well, as I said, I can't reveal any information about any of the hotel's guests, but since this is sort of non-information, it should be okay."

"Good. I wouldn't want you to do anything that could get you in trouble with your job."

"Right. Unfortunately, there were too many records to go through individually, but there was something that set one of our guests apart from the others. I don't know if this is the same person you're looking for, but it just seemed sort of strange."

Abby held her breath, hoping—and with a little prayer thrown in there for good measure—that this tidbit of "non-information" as Cheryl had called it would help lead her to at least one of the baby's parents.

"Anyway, this customer arrived in the middle of the Flashback Festival and stayed for a little over a week, but he paid for his room, day to day, with *cash*. Who pays for stuff with cash nowadays?" She paused as if she were trying to find the answer to her own question. "All the other guests paid with a credit card, traveler's checks or debit cards. And there's one other thing."

Abby doodled a dollar sign on her note pad. "What's that?"

"Even if I told you his name, it wouldn't do you any good. Both his first and last names are so common that you'd never be able to find him without an address or credit card to go on."

"John Smith?" Abby ventured.

"Close enough."

"He obviously didn't want to be found," she said.

"Just thought you'd like to know so you don't end up chasing any dead ends," Cheryl said.

"Thanks for telling me." Abby pushed the quarterly report to the edge of her desk and picked up her duty sheet for the Skills and Crafts fundraiser. "I'll focus my energy elsewhere."

Like tomorrow's walkathon.

THE PLAN HAD BEEN to just eat cookies, drink tea, laugh and enjoy each other's company, Ellen thought. Simple as that. But sometimes God added layers to people's simple plans, and today was one such day.

It quickly became clear that God was using her newly strengthened friendship with Terza so that Ellen might bring her comfort. Another possibility occurred to her, one in which He might be using their friendship to push Ellen to find closure.

As Moses lay on her lap, Terza stroked his fuzzy black hair, pushing it to one side as if she were combing it with her hand. "Zhi Ming was our first and only child," she said, her eyes glazing over as she went back in her memory. "We had a good life in Hong Kong before he came along. Good jobs, a beautiful apartment and much love for each other."

She blushed slightly as she said that last part, and Ellen recalled that, other than occasional handholding, she and Martin rarely expressed their affection in public. But even without those blatant signs, anyone could tell that they were deeply in love with each other.

"Our love grew into a beautiful blossom that was the boy God gave us. This little flower bloomed for only a short season."

"I knew that you'd had a child," Ellen said, "but I'd never heard how you lost him."

"That's because this is the first I have spoken of it," she said. For a moment, Terza sat so still that she looked like a delicately sculpted figurine. "He was two years old, almost three," she said at last. "Almost Beau's age. A beautiful little boy, just like our young friend."

Ellen smiled, remembering Beau's happy giggles. His face was different because of the cleft in his lip, but he was indeed beautiful. She imagined a Chinese version of Beau and that was how she pictured little Zhi Ming.

"Martin was a wonderful father." Terza thumped her chest with her fist and smiled. "So proud! Every day he would rush home from work to play with our son. I will never forget Zhi Ming's squeals and laughter when his daddy came home."

It was as if Terza had described a scene from Ellen's own past. Mary racing Abby to be the first to greet George at the door. Abby as a toddler sitting on George's truck fender, "helping" her dad change the oil. Ellen's throat tightened at the memory. There should also have been—

"In our apartment was a magnificent lacquer chest given to us by Martin's grandfather. He had made it himself with paintings of cherry trees and sweethearts walking over an arched bridge in a glorious garden."

By now Moses had stopped wiggling on her lap. It seemed as though he, too, was listening with rapt attention.

"There were pull drawers on the bottom, and the shelves on

top were covered with hinged doors. I kept a music box up there on the top shelf. Zhi Ming always wanted me to play it, over and over." Terza paused to hum a few notes, the tune lilting and delicate. "One day, after the twentieth time of winding it up, I said, 'Enough. Time to take a bath.' I went to start the water flowing. One minute he was right behind me and it was only seconds later when I heard a heavy crash."

Ellen sucked in her breath, hurting for her friend, yet not knowing quite what to say. And another part of her was amazed that Terza was able to recall what had happened without crumpling into a distressed heap.

"He had pulled the bottom drawers out to climb up to the top," she said. "His weight threw the chest off balance and it fell on top of him. There was nothing I could do. He died on the way to the hospital."

Although Terza had remained stoic, Ellen couldn't hold back the tears. The couple had gone through all of this, and yet they were two of the most cheerful and God-loving people she knew.

"He's asleep," Terza said, scooping her hands under the baby's body.

As she laid him in the bassinet, Ellen rose from her chair. The two women stood side by side staring down into the bed of the child that had, in his own mysterious way, been a catalyst for the story that had just unfolded here this afternoon.

It was common knowledge that Martin and Terza had never had more children. But even more common was the knowledge that the couple had turned their love toward others who came into their lives. Visitors to their bed-and-breakfast often responded so strongly to that love that some of them kept in touch with letters and Christmas cards even years later.

Ellen thanked God for bringing Terza and Martin to

Sparrow Island, and for giving the women this opportunity to learn more about each other. And, in light of what she had just learned, she silently thanked God for the two wonderful daughters He had given her.

Turning toward Terza, she held open her arms. The women drew toward each other, clinging to the comfort that each had to offer. The tears flowed, but Terza's were not tears of regret. In fact, they seemed like tears of joy at having, at long last, found someone with whom to share this piece of her past.

After a moment, Terza drew away. Taking a tissue from the box that had been placed near the bassinet, she handed one to Ellen and took another for herself.

After they'd wiped away the tears, Terza cleared any lingering sadness from her voice. "It's not up to me to judge or ask why," she said softly. "My job is to have faith that God is in control and that I must trust Him with what happens in the rest of my life."

She gripped Ellen by the shoulders and gave her a meaningful smile.

"But in the meantime, He has given me other children to love. Little ones at church. Guests at the inn. And now, Moses."

Ellen lifted her gaze and gave Terza's arm a comforting squeeze. Somehow, though the comfort had been meant for her friend, it came back to her, filling her own heart with a sense of peace.

She wanted to tell Terza her story. Let her know that she was not alone in her loss. But not now. Not while the revelation of Terza's own story was still so fresh and fragile.

CHAPTER ✿ TWELVE

Tuesday morning Mary slid the leather gloves onto her hands and flexed her fingers. The padding on the palms might not completely protect her from blisters, but it would greatly reduce the chance of developing tender spots.

They were a couple of hours early for the walkathon, and the church parking lot was still empty except for her and Henry. The clear sky promised a warm day, but a breeze from the sound would likely keep them cool. Just to be sure, Mary had worn a thin gauzy skirt and a cap sleeved top.

According to her sister's calculations, the first of the walkers should overtake her shortly after she left the park and turned onto Kingfisher Avenue. Mary had laughed when Abby had suggested timing her on a quarter-mile practice run so that she could anticipate a general timeframe for finishing. Then when Abby had pulled out her calculator and started converting from miles to kilometers and adjusting for rough terrain and fatigue, Mary couldn't hold back the giggles. It was so like Abby to take such a scientific approach to something as basic as pushing a wheelchair. Fortunately, Abby had been a good sport and had laughed along with her. When she'd suggested beginning an hour and forty-eight minutes before the children's scheduled starting time, Mary had lost it and laughed until she got hiccups.

Henry rubbed his hands together. "Are you sure you're up for this?"

"Yep, I'm ready," Mary insisted. "How about you?"

Dressed in shorts, sneakers and a beige and brown pullover shirt, Henry had also donned the utility belt from his uniform. Spare bottles of water hung from the belt and he'd thoughtfully dropped some bandages into the tote bag that hung beside Mary's chair.

He grinned. "Couldn't be more ready. I've been working out by chasing criminals so that you won't get too far ahead of me."

Amused, Mary squeezed his hand. Since crime on the islands was very low, that was certainly an overstatement.

Finnegan sensed the excitement and made a couple of half-starts to indicate he was ready to be moving. "Look at him," Mary said. "The way he acts, you'd think he was still a puppy."

"I know how that is," Henry said, rubbing a palm over his bald dome. "If I had more hair, folks would think I was still in my thirties."

Mary smiled at this amazing man that God had brought into her life. When his job called for it, he could be as serious and hardnosed as needed. But when it was just the two of them, he usually showed her his softer and funnier side.

Finnegan broke into her thoughts with a sound that, on a human, she would have described as a mumble.

"Okay, okay, I hear you," Mary said with a laugh as she grasped the wheel rims and gave a push.

Henry moved behind her to give her some help over the gravel and up onto the sidewalk, but once she was past those initial obstacles she urged him to walk beside her.

When they passed Island Blooms on Shoreline Drive, Henry pointed to a large hand-lettered sign in the window of the flower shop declaring GO, MARY! The lettering was covered with colored marker drawings of vines and blossoms. Inside, Candace peeked out the window and, seeing her, flung open the door.

Her waist-length strawberry blonde hair streamed behind her as she ran outside to greet Mary. Throwing her arms around her neck, the petite thirty-something woman excitedly proclaimed, "I'm so proud of you, Mary. You're my inspiration!" Then, as if she realized that her gushing display of emotion might be a little embarrassing, she immediately straightened and added, "Hey, since you're going over to Kingfisher Avenue and Primrose Lane anyway, do you want to make a few deliveries along the way?"

The joke was met with hearty guffaws from both Mary and Henry. A bit of a back-to-nature artsy type, Candace had had to learn a few business skills when Mary had promoted her to manage the flower shop. In fact, she'd turned out to have keen insights into ways to improve business and cut costs. So Mary couldn't help dishing a little of the teasing back at her.

"Been reading time management books during your down time?"

"I wish we had a little down time," the young woman said as she opened the shop door. "Lots of work to do, so I'd better get on it. Be safe!" she cautioned and disappeared inside with a jangle of the bell on the door.

The first leg of the route along Shoreline Drive proved to be fairly easy. Other than a couple of places where tree roots were beginning to push up through the sidewalk, the course was smooth. When they got to the entrance to the public park, Henry helped her across the road. Because he'd been concerned that motorists might not notice her, he had attached a long stick with a yellow flag on it to her chair. Every so often, Mary could hear the fabric flap over her head when the breeze caught the triangular shaped flag.

Although she had resisted Henry's help earlier, Mary entertained second thoughts by the time she'd crossed the grassy area where the concert had been held a few nights ago. It wasn't until they'd reached the bike path that circled the park that she began to question her stubbornness in insisting on doing it completely by herself.

She stopped the chair and rubbed her arms.

"Tired?" Henry placed his beefy hands on her shoulders and massaged gently. "You know, there's nothing wrong with accepting a little help when the going gets rough."

Mary placed her gloved hands on top of his and turned her cheek so that it rested against his kneading fingers.

"No, I'm okay. It looked like Finnegan needed a break."

Although the dog was eight years old, middle-aged in canine years, he still had plenty of spunk. As if to prove her wrong, he danced his hindquarters around as a sign that he was anxious to keep moving.

The scent of the moist earth and ground-covering ferns pleased Mary's senses, making her wish she had time to take her Bible meditation right here in the outdoors, as was Abby's habit. It was plain to see why her sister felt closer to God when she was outdoors. And if it was this pleasing to humans, then how much more fun for a dog who could detect the lingering presence of squirrels, rabbits, foxes, lizards and other things that would be fun to chase.

"Right," Henry said, gently mocking her. Even so, he reached into the tote bag beside her chair to retrieve a collapsible bowl. Then, unfastening one of the bottles of water from his belt, he poured out some for Finnegan and gave another bottle to Mary.

After they'd all quenched their thirst, they set off again, but soon Mary couldn't use the dog as her excuse for stopping. She was breathing hard and her arms were aching. To make matters worse, the occasional vines, rocks and tree roots that would barely slow a bicycle were proving to be an impediment to her slower moving chariot.

She stopped again, knowing that if she didn't keep moving the children would soon overtake her and beat her to the picnic at the Emorys' by a large margin.

"Your mom is accepting help taking care of Moses," Henry reminded her. "That doesn't make her less of a foster mother."

"Of course it doesn't," Mary agreed.

"And when one of the kids in the Skills and Crafts group has a tough time putting up the badminton net by himself, do you tell him to just try harder?"

She snorted. "No, I suggest he get one of the other kids to . . ." Mary twisted in her chair to peer at the man who was challenging her thinking. "I see where you're going with this."

That didn't matter to Henry, who obviously wanted to drive home his point with one more illustration. "And when someone at church is going through a tough personal time, does Rev. Hale tell them to just bear up under the burden?"

"No," Mary said, grinning at her boyfriend's persistence. He knew just which buttons to push to get her to change her mind. "He would tell them to turn to God for help."

"Exactly. And since the help you need right now is physical rather than spiritual, He sent me," Henry said, rubbing the top of his head. "So keep in mind that if you turn down my offer of help, you're turning both of us down."

"You really know how to build a case, don't you?" Mary leaned forward to give the wheels an extra bit of muscle while he pushed from behind. His chuckle seemed to fall around her in a caress.

THAT SAME DAY, after Abby had taken the birders back to The Bird Nest, she drove straight to the park to meet Hugo at the Skills and Crafts group's midpoint "watering hole."

The group leaders had considered holding the event on a Saturday, but given the extra traffic from weekend tourists, it had been decided Tuesday would be a safer choice. And since the children were out of school for the summer anyway, they were glad for the midweek diversion.

Hugo stepped out from his post behind the refreshment table. "From your smile, I take it today went better than yesterday?"

She nodded, pleased with how things had turned out. "I was able to talk the feuding friends into attending class again. The good news is that, even though they avoided each other at first, they actually seem to be making strides in repairing their friendship."

Hugo paused and ran a finger over his white mustache. "And the bad news is?"

"Well, the 'other' news is that the cousins are still claiming to have made two very rare sightings in the past week. My gut says to disregard it, but I don't want to dismiss such an unusual report if what they say is true."

He laid a hand on her shoulder. "I have no doubt that you'll do the right thing."

Abby filled several paper cups with ice from the cooler and helped herself to one. "The drinks look untouched. I take it that means the kids haven't been past here yet?"

"Ever the sleuth, you are. And once again you're right." He arranged cups and ice on the table. "Mary came and went with Henry a short while ago, and the first of the kids should catch up with her by the time she reaches the library."

After some convincing last night, Mary had agreed that it would be wise to take a bit of a head start so she'd get to Vince's house in time for the post-walk cookout and games with the children. It was only after she'd talked to Henry on the phone that she acknowledged a head start wasn't cheating, given that she'd be covering the same distance as the others.

And Henry, sweetheart that he was, had arranged to take a few hours off to walk the course with her. And, of course, give her chair a little nudge over tree roots and other obstacles if necessary. But Mary had made him promise that he wouldn't give her any help unless she asked for it.

"Bobby McDonald and José Bondevik were fighting for the lead as they entered the park's walking trail," Hugo added. "The trees are in the way, so I haven't been able to follow their progress. I'm just waiting to see who'll come out first."

Since Abby had helped Mary with some of the route planning, she knew that adult volunteers had been stationed at various points along the walkathon course, including the tree-edged path around the park, to assure the children's safety.

"They're neck-and-neck?" Abby asked. "But José's several inches taller than Bobby and very athletic."

Hugo grinned. "Yeah, you should have seen Bobby's legs churning. That kid was kicking up dust, I tell you. He's determined to win that prize for being the first to complete the course."

And the prize for gathering the most sponsors, Abby recalled. She wondered what other prizes he might be competing for.

They waited together, pouring water from liter bottles into the ice-filled cups in preparation for the thirsty walkers who would soon descend upon the table.

In another few minutes, Wyatt Kelser emerged from the wooded path. Abby recognized the ten-year-old by his flaming red hair. Three others followed him out, and the small group sprinted toward the refreshment table, playfully shoving each other to be the first to grab a drink.

Concerned, Abby looked up at Hugo. "Didn't you say that Bobby and José were in the lead?"

He frowned and rubbed his forehead. "Yes, but there's no way they could have taken a wrong turn. Not with the chaperones along the path directing which way to go."

By this time Wyatt had reached the table, but despite his exertion and hard breathing, he didn't go directly to the drinks. Instead, he went straight to Hugo and pointed back toward the walking trail.

"Somebody bit the dust," he said through ragged breaths. The kids who came behind him added their own renditions, which included words like *splatter* and *kablooie*.

Glad that she still had her comfortable birding clothes on, Abby took off to the section of the trail where the children had emerged a moment ago. Now little Hillary Storm jogged out with a couple of her friends. When the seven-year-old saw Abby running full out across the park lawn, she turned back and pointed the way.

Abby's heart clenched. If a seven-year-old girl had passed Bobby, then something must be terribly wrong. His pride— and lately his highly competitive spirit—wouldn't have let him come in after a girl three years younger than himself.

She had just entered the oak and maple shaded trail when Patricia Hale came around the bend with José and Bobby. Favoring his right leg, José limped toward her, supported by the preacher's wife on one side and Bobby on the other. The boy leaned heavily on Bobby's shoulder. The heels of his hands were scraped, as well as his knees, and he was trying his hardest to put on a brave front.

"I think he's going to be fine," Patricia quickly assured her, though Abby wondered how much of that was for José's ears. Patricia's tone and attitude were very calming for everyone within earshot. "He's got a few scrapes and bumps, but they look worse than they really are."

"I'm so glad to hear that," Abby said, falling into step beside Patricia as they crossed the grassy area toward the snack table. "Bobby, how about you? Are you okay?"

He nodded resolutely, but it was clear he wasn't happy with the situation.

Patricia quietly filled in the details. "I saw the whole thing. Bobby was beginning to pull rather far ahead. That's when José decided to put it in high gear. Unfortunately, his ankle twisted and he went for a tumble." She lowered her voice even further. "I don't think it's broken because he was walking on it before I got to him, but he might have a bit of a sprain."

"You go ahead," José urged his friend. "I'll be all right."

Bobby shook his head and adjusted his grip around José's waist. "Nah."

The boy winced briefly as he mistakenly tried to put weight on his injured ankle, but he quickly tried to deflect their concern. Directing his comment to Bobby, he said, "I wonder if they'll give a prize for last place?"

Bobby shrugged. "You're welcome to that one."

By the time they reached the break station, Hugo had pulled out a folding chair and scattered the contents of his first aid kit on the table.

While he tended to José, Abby poured drinks for all of them, then pulled Bobby aside. "That was a nice thing you did," she said, "giving up the lead to help your friend."

He lifted one corner of his mouth, the motion causing a dimple to form in his cheek. "I was in first place," he said, ignoring her compliment. "The prize for the first place winner is a kit for growing sea monkeys." He clenched his fist. "And I really wanted that."

Abby put her arm around his scrawny shoulder. "I know. But at least you still have a chance at winning the prize for having the most sponsors," she said in an effort to console him.

But *consoled* was not the expression that crossed his freckled face. He shrugged and pulled away.

Bobby pushed his hands through the front of his hair, causing his short brown hair to stand up in awkward spikes. "I'm not gonna win that either."

Abby frowned as he toyed with an empty paper cup before tossing it into the garbage and shoving his hands into his shorts pockets.

"I don't understand," she pressed. "You had pages and pages of sponsors signed up. Way more than any of the other kids."

He looked away, refusing to meet her gaze. "I found a linkhole."

A *linkhole*? That was a new one to her. She wondered if he meant he'd found a shortcut through the walkathon course. "You mean a hole in a chain-link fence?"

"No," he said, a little impatient that she wasn't following. "An easy way to win that's not exactly cheating, but it's not totally square either."

He sighed heavily. It was plain that this had been difficult for him to admit, and Abby admired his forthrightness in doing so.

"I thought about our memory verse for this week," he continued, "and I don't want God to be mad at me when He finds out."

Abby suppressed a smile and the urge to remind him that God already knew whatever he was about to reveal. "Which memory verse is that?"

"Proverbs 10:9. 'The man of integrity walks securely, but he who takes crooked paths will be found out.'"

"Oh." Abby straightened as she began to understand what he'd been trying to tell her. "Why don't you tell me about this *loophole* of yours?"

MARY AND HENRY were in sight of The Tackle Shop when the first of the group overtook them. Although she'd teased Abby for her analytical approach to calculating the starting time, she had to concede that her little sister had been very close on her estimate.

Brenda Wilson was scooping out ice cream for the walkers and got so carried away with the fun of it that she began offering some to customers going into the store and even passersby on the sidewalk. Mary asked for strawberry with a drizzle of chocolate on top, and Henry opted for plain vanilla.

While they ate and Mary gave her arms a longed-for rest, she was surprised to see that Bobby wasn't among the children milling and talking in front of the store. Mary assumed he and José were intent on being the first to arrive at Vince and Cheryl Emory's house and had barely stopped to grab a cone before they were off again.

"Don't worry," Brenda assured her and Henry. "I've stationed Chad at the corner to act as crossing guard. He'll make sure they all get across Primrose Lane safely."

Mary had no doubt about that. Brenda's son, a mechanical engineering college student, was one of the most conscientious people she knew. Even when he was still in high school, he had approached Henry for guidance on acquiring his emergency medical technician certificate.

The Skills and Crafts kids who had lagged behind knew they wouldn't be the first to cross the finish line, so they had decided to stop and socialize before tackling the last mile.

Young Hillary put a hand to her forehead. "Ooh, ice cream headache."

"Bet it doesn't hurt as bad as José's ankle," Bryan said in an attempt to one-up her.

"Or as much as losing because of José's disaster," Willow chimed in. "Boy, I bet Bobby's ticked about missing out on that sea monkey prize for first place."

Mary almost dropped her ice cream cone. "Disaster? What happened?"

As they excitedly tried to outtalk each other in describing the "bloody carnage" of José's knees and hands, Henry yanked the remaining bottle of water off his belt and was preparing to run back to the park. It was only when Hillary insisted that José was no longer there—that Patricia Hale had taken him to the Medical Center to be checked out—that Henry stopped.

"Bobby rode with them to the doctor's so José wouldn't be scared," Hillary said with a sigh of admiration. "He's so thoughtful."

After a bit more prying and pointed questions, Mary discovered the "bloody carnage" had merely been a couple of scraped knees, and that Patricia suspected José might have sprained his ankle and was only taking him to the doctor as a precaution.

"I think we should pray about it," the precocious Hillary said. "You said any time our friends are hurt or in trouble, we should pray."

Henry grinned at Mary, obviously impressed that the messages taught in the Skills and Crafts group actually stuck.

Mary couldn't have been more proud if it had been her own grandchild who'd offered up such a simple and caring suggestion. "That's lovely Hillary," Mary said. "Why don't we all offer up a silent prayer for José."

WHILE MARY FINISHED her ice cream, Henry walked over and said something to Bryan. The boy nodded and tossed his napkin into the trash can before heading out to finish the final distance to the Emorys' where food and an above-ground pool awaited them. Then Henry asked for a second cone, which Brenda heaped with chocolate ice cream.

"Worked up an appetite, did you?" Mary teased.

But he didn't eat it himself. As they approached the intersection of Kingfisher and Primrose, Chad stepped out into the narrow street and stopped a couple of cars by waving a red cloth. With a "Thanks, bud," Henry handed the grateful young man the overloaded ice cream cone.

The final leg of the course was the hardest. Mary's arms burned from the effort, but she refused to let Henry give her a push. With each forward thrust against the rim of the wheels, she thanked God for something. Even Henry got into it, and they took turns calling out a gratitude.

"My strong arms," Mary said.

"A sturdy wheelchair," Henry added.

She laughed. "Leave it to a man to remember the vehicle." Then, more seriously, she said, "Henry, who means so much to me."

Walking beside her, he kissed his hand, then touched it to her cheek. "My sweet, funny, lovable Mary."

They continued on like that for a while, with the straggling walkers passing her along the way. Their little game actually made the time seem to pass more quickly. They were having so much fun that by the time they reached the Emory property, she almost hated for it to end. Almost, but not quite. Her arms burned furiously as she rolled across the grassy front yard, and she thanked God for the blessing of finishing the walkathon, even though they were the last ones to arrive.

A couple of the kids who'd been out front spotted them, then immediately ran to the backyard. They returned a few seconds later with the rest of the children and all the adult leaders.

Bryan handed Hillary one end of a roll of yellow streamer paper, and they stretched it out in front of Mary and Henry like a finish line tape. The others stood on either side calling out encouragement and cheering them on.

Mary tried to push through the grassy front yard, but emotion and fatigue overwhelmed her. With the back of her wrist, she brushed away the mist that suddenly clouded her vision.

"Oh my," she said to Henry. "Look at those little darlings!"

All this time she'd been encouraging them with their special projects and applauding their successes. Now the children were returning the loving support to her and it felt so sweet that Mary could barely breathe from the sheer joy of it.

Smiling through the hazy tears that filled her eyes, Mary forced her aching arms and back to keep going for just a few more yards. Then her wheel got stuck on one of the zillions of rocks that made up Sparrow Island and she struggled unsuccessfully for a few seconds.

"Come on Mary!" Bryan shouted. "We know you can do it."

Henry moved behind her and bent so that his lips were close to her ear. "Are you ready for that push now?"

"Yeah," she said. "Let's go in blazing."

Henry gave a mighty shove, running the rest of the way to the finish line.

At the last instant, Mary lifted her weary arms and the tape fell away behind her.

CHAPTER ❦ THIRTEEN

When Terza returned to the Stanton farm Wednesday afternoon, she and Ellen settled into what was now becoming a familiar routine. Feed, then play with the baby until he grew sleepy enough for his nap. Then settle down to tea sipped from the nearly century-old silver set that had been handed down to Ellen from her mother's side of the family.

They sat side by side on the couch, their knees touching as they bent their heads together over the small photo album that Terza had brought today.

"Thank you for trusting me with your story. I wish I could have known Zhi Ming," Ellen said as she touched the faded color photograph. If he had lived, he would be just a few years older than Ida Tolliver. "I imagine that if he were with us today, he would have Martin's strength and honor." She smiled. "And your kindness and sense of style."

Terza didn't look up from the photo of the black-haired child showing an uneven row of baby teeth to the camera. A young woman with long black hair—obviously Terza—lay on her back on a bamboo floor mat, holding the child up over her. The upper corner of the shot revealed a portion of a man's finger, as if Martin had been gesturing to the mother and child as he took their picture.

Ellen observed her friend and noted a sheen of brightness to her eyes that hadn't been there when she had told her yesterday what had happened almost a quarter of a century ago.

Reaching out, she touched Terza's arm. "Are you okay?"

Terza blinked, then wiped her face with her hand. "Yes, very much okay. I feel better after our talk yesterday." She leaned back against the couch cushions and looked straight ahead. "Sometimes it feels like it's not real," she said placing a hand on the album to indicate that part of her life. "It's like I made it up. Made *him* up."

With an understanding that filled Ellen until her chest ached, she knew too well what Terza meant. It was the reason she had pressed so hard to keep Moses on the island with her. She didn't want him to cease to exist in the way that Terza had described.

"Talking about Zhi Ming yesterday made him real again."

Ellen wasn't sure who reached out first, but soon their hands were clasped, fingers tightening together in a way that symbolized the new and stronger interweaving of their lives.

After a moment, Ellen leaned forward to peek at the baby in the bassinet, but he hadn't stirred in some time.

Terza flipped the page to a studio shot of the little boy, now older and wearing a "big boy" outfit of a white shirt and black shorts held up by suspenders.

Ellen's hips were getting stiff, so she got up to cover the

Chocolate Wonder cake that Sandy McDonald had brought over last night. "You know, I've been thinking about Zhi Ming a lot since yesterday," she said as she puttered around the coffee table. "In fact, there's something I'd like to tell you."

Just as the words came out of her mouth, an uneasy feeling crept up her spine. She tried to shake it away, but it wouldn't leave. Ellen felt her heart thumping against her chest, as if she'd taken a flight of stairs too quickly. It was as if she knew something was wrong, but she didn't know what.

"Yes?" Terza said, urging her on.

Reflexively, Ellen moved to the bassinet. When she looked in it, her knees almost buckled. The baby was blue.

"Something's wrong," she said, her voice sounding more calm than she felt inside. She reached in to snatch him up. "Something's wrong!"

Terza leaped to her feet, the photo album falling to the floor. "What is it?"

Just as she'd been taught in the foster parent training class, Ellen held the limp baby in her arms so that his head tipped slightly back to open the airway. Placing her face close to his mouth, she couldn't detect any airflow.

"He's not breathing. Call the paramedics!"

Vaguely aware that Terza had rushed to the phone in the kitchen, Ellen gave the child two quick puffs from her cheeks and paused to see if the action stimulated his breathing.

It had not. If anything, he was turning an even darker shade of blue.

Ellen turned toward the coffee table and knelt down in front of it. With the back of one arm, she swept the heirloom tea set from the table with a clatter of teapot, cups and spilled tea and proceeded to administer CPR.

WALKING AROUND Oyster Inlet was exactly what Abby needed this morning. At eight o'clock, the morning mist still clung thickly to the sky, making it feel as though the group of birders was wrapped in layers of gauze.

A light hat and jacket protected Abby's head and body from the floating dew, but the cold waves at the edge of the rocky shore invaded her water shoes and kept her from getting too lost in her thoughts.

Warren and Conrad were unusually quiet this morning, which was okay with her. She had taken them both aside to inform them that she wanted them to accompany her when she made her report to the birding society tomorrow. Perhaps a few well-targeted questions from the group's representative might help get to the bottom of the unusual sightings they claimed to have made.

Right now, however, Abby was more concerned about her mother and baby Moses. She and Terza had done a terrific job of reviving the infant yesterday afternoon, and they had all given prayers of thanks that the women's quick actions had resulted in a good prognosis for his health.

Ellen had performed the infant CPR, giving two cheek-puffs for every fifteen chest compressions with her fingers. While she had taken care of that, Terza had called the paramedics. Rather than wait for the crew to come to the farm, Terza had insisted on meeting them at the station, which was directly on the way to the Medical Center. From there, the trained professionals took over, moving the child to an ambulance and racing up Municipal Street with the siren squealing.

Amazingly, Moses had come through as if nothing had happened at all. As of last night, when Dr. Randolph had released him to return home with Ellen and George, the baby had been in incredible condition. Abby and Mary had stayed with their parents until Moses was back on his normal eating and sleeping schedule and their parents assured them that they would be able to manage him through the night.

Between that crisis and the excitement of the walkathon the day before, Abby was exhausted, but she was glad to be out in her element.

A movement some distance away on the water caught her eye. Abby lifted the binoculars to her face, knowing the others in the party would follow suit. Out there, bobbing along on a bed of floating kelp, stood a solitary great blue heron, very common in the San Juans. The four-foot-tall bird posed like an offshore sentry, clearly visible despite the ribbons of mist that wafted through the air.

"Unlike other tall birds, when herons are in flight they continue to hold their necks in an *S*-shaped curve," she told the group. "These birds have special patches of powder-down feathers that are so brittle they disintegrate when touched by the heron's bill."

She lowered the binoculars and let them dangle from her neck.

"You can't see it from here, but the heron's center toe is serrated like a comb. After he's finished preening and spreading the feather dust through his plumage, he'll rake his toes over the feathers to comb out the excess dust."

Though the rest of the birders contributed comments or asked questions, Jenny and Charlotte stayed quietly on the periphery of the group. Abby was glad to see that they were murmuring to each other—a huge improvement in their friendship since last weekend—but they didn't seem to be very much into the bird-watching today.

Word had spread quickly, especially after Janet got the prayer team involved in praying for the baby's recovery. Jenny's name was on the prayer chain list, so Abby assumed she must have been informed about yesterday's emergency.

As they moved toward their next venue, a wooded blind area up on the rocks where they could watch the shy little Harlequin ducks dive for breakfast, Abby slowed to speak to the two women. Before she could give the update as of late last night, Jenny had jumped right into the subject.

"Please tell me that our prayers were answered," she pleaded. "Little Moses has been on my heart all night. I barely slept at all."

Judging by the rings under her eyes, Abby would have known that even without her saying so. She smiled and put an arm around the woman's shoulder as they walked.

"No one knows why he stopped breathing," Abby said. "The doctor indicated that if the worst had happened and Mom hadn't been able to revive him, it would have been classified as SIDS, which is Sudden Infant Death Syndrome." When Jenny's face paled, Abby quickly added, "He's fine now. When I saw him last night, you couldn't even tell he'd been through a trauma. Of course, the heart monitor would have given it away, but that's mainly for my parents' peace of mind."

Throughout their conversation, Charlotte hadn't said a word. In fact, she almost looked bored with the conversation.

Abby stepped aside and retrieved the cell phone from her bag. Good, there were lots of bars on the phone's status line.

"Excuse me a moment. I want to call my mother while we still have a good signal and see how Moses is doing this morning. You all can go ahead and I'll catch up in a minute."

As the phone rang on the other end, Abby recalled the

amazing sense of calm that had surrounded her mother and Terza when she'd met them at the hospital yesterday. Despite the shock of what they'd dealt with in getting the child to the Medical Center, the two women had repeated "He'll be fine" as if they knew it with a certainty. And Ellen had kept saying something about being given a second chance.

Abby was grateful for that second chance that God had given the little boy. At less than two weeks old, he'd already been through so much.

When Ellen picked up the phone, Abby was quick to note that her mother's voice was calm and cheerful. "How are things going this morning? Since Mary and I didn't hear from you, we assumed you had an uneventful night."

"Yes, indeed. Moses slept like a baby." Ellen interrupted herself to laugh at her own joke. "However, your dad and I took turns setting the alarm to get up and check on him."

"You must be exhausted. Why don't I come over tonight and give you a break?" She had no doubt her mother was still wearing the baby sling that Terza had made for her. Just carrying the baby around with her all day would be enough to tire her out.

"Thank you, dear, but that's not necessary. Dr. Randolph said the monitor would alert us if he were to stop breathing again. We just wanted to be extra careful last night, at least until we felt confident that the machine would do its job."

Abby sighed her relief. Even though she didn't know much about caring for infants, she would have canceled the birding class this morning to go and help her mother. But last night as she was leaving the farm to go home with Mary, George had insisted that he would forgo his farming duties for the day to provide an extra pair of watchful eyes over the baby.

"It'll probably feel like a vacation when you go back to your part-time job at the Visitors Center next week," Abby joked. Then, abruptly, her attention was jerked away. "I have to go now. One of the guys hollered something about a tufted puffin, but I suspect it's an auklet instead. I'll see you later."

When Abby caught up to the group, she found that the bird in question was indeed a rhinoceros auklet, which was very common at this time of year. Once again, it was Conrad who had seen the bird first, this time claiming it was a puffin. This led her to further suspect the cousins' other reports.

After she'd set them straight, she quickly told Jenny and Charlotte that Moses had done well and that the heart monitor hadn't gone off the entire night.

"That's wonderful," Jenny said. "I was so worried about him."

Charlotte took the news with bland disinterest, which Jenny construed as a challenge to get her friend as excited as she was over Moses' successful night.

"You talked about wanting to adopt him," Jenny urged. "You must be happy that he's better now."

With a shrug of her shoulder, Charlotte dismissed her friend's enthusiasm. "I'm glad he's going to be okay, but I've changed my mind about wanting to adopt him. It's hard enough trying to raise a healthy kid, so I sure don't want to take on a problem child."

Stunned, Abby turned and stared at the woman, appalled at her obvious self-centeredness. She wanted to say something— anything—to make Charlotte realize how hurtful her words were, but most of all how much she would miss out on in life if she only associated with people who didn't seem to have any troubles.

But before she could form the words, Jenny picked up her dual-purpose, three-legged chair and folded it into a walking stick. For a moment, Abby feared Jenny might bop her clueless friend over the head with it, but she just thumped it against the dirt for emphasis.

"Honestly, Charlotte, I can't believe that anyone can be so callous." Then she stalked away and joined the older sisters who were taking pictures of the auklet.

"What?" Charlotte called out after her. When she got only Jenny's angrily turned back as a response, she turned to Abby. "What did I say?"

THAT EVENING, Abby and Mary made their way over to Stanton Farm to bring Ellen and George dinner.

As Abby gave Mary a push up the ramp to the front door, she asked "Is the soreness gone from your arms yet?"

The night of the walkathon, Abby had helped ice her sister's aching arms. Although Finnegan had happily walked the entire course with her and Henry, Mary had refused to ask her dog to help pull her as he might have done under ordinary circumstances involving, perhaps, an upward sloping sidewalk.

Mary flexed an arm and squeezed her bicep. "Yeah, it's still a little tender, but it's eased up some. The trick is to keep using the muscles to keep them from tightening up even further."

Two additional cars were parked in the driveway: Terza's and Joanne's. She assumed both women popped in to check on Moses as well as her parents.

Inside, Joanne stood near the door, holding a couple of pillowcase sacks. She'd been dropping by almost every day, staying only fifteen minutes or so. Sometimes she brought food, but mostly she just picked up the laundry to wash and return the next time she came. Although she lived next door, it made sense to drive her car over to the twenty-five-acre property since she would be struggling to handle both the heavy laundry sack and an active toddler.

Abby had taken care of her parent's laundry since she knew which pieces they liked starched and ironed and which were okay to just fold and stack. She was glad Joanne had been able to help with the baby's things, which needed to be turned around more quickly.

Beau, of course, was nowhere near his foster mother. True to his curious nature, he stood by the empty bassinet and pointed to various parts of the monitoring equipment, asking, "What's 'at?"

Then, satisfied that all his questions had been answered, he went over to where Ellen sat in her favorite chair and leaned over the arm to peek at the baby nestled in her arms. He said something that Abby couldn't understand, but Joanne interpreted it to mean, "I big."

"His speech will get better after he has more surgery," Joanne explained. "Under ideal circumstances, the child welfare people would like for him to be securely established in a permanent family first. If no one steps forward to adopt him soon, though, we'll have to schedule it while he's with us."

"Being that little pitchers have big ears, we probably shouldn't do it now," Ellen said, trying to phrase her statement in a way that wouldn't cause little toddler antennae to perk up, "but let's all pray about the situation. Everyone needs a permanent place to belong."

Finnegan rose and turned to watch the door, his tail wagging furiously.

A moment later, Henry entered the room, taking off his

hat. "What a nice surprise," he joked. "You folks didn't need to throw a party just because I was coming."

He walked over to Mary and, after bending down to pat the ecstatic dog, he held her hand. Abby grinned at the way her sister lit up whenever Henry was near.

"Actually, I was just in the area, so I thought I'd drop by to check on Moses." After Ellen and George assured him that the baby was doing fine, he got down to the other reason for showing up unannounced. "We've talked to everyone at the Senior Center, but no one knows anything that we haven't already dug up on our own."

Although Abby was on pins and needles to ask him a few specific questions of her own, she patiently held her tongue.

"Oh, and by the way," he said, turning to Abby, "when we requested The Dorset's hotel records to check the guest register, Cheryl Emory mentioned that you'd already been there."

"Our Abby doesn't waste much time," Ellen said benignly.

Abby didn't try to deny that curiosity and hope had driven her to find out what she could even though she knew the sheriff's department was staying on top of the case. "You didn't have much luck there either, did you?"

He shook his head and ran a hand over its bald top. "A cash customer and a generic name were all we got. It was a total dead end."

For some reason, Abby suddenly didn't feel so bad for having struck out there as well. Yet, it still would have been nice if he'd found something that would lead them to Moses' birth parents.

By now, Beau was bored with the baby and was yanking on Joanne's arm as she listened in on their conversation.

She stiffened her arm to brace against his pulling. "Wait a

minute, honey." Turning to Henry, she asked, "Are you close to finding the parents?"

He playfully placed his hat on Beau's head and chuckled as the little boy paraded around, showing off for the others and then draping the hat over the dog's eyes. Finnegan tolerated the attention in good humor.

"It's not looking good," he said glumly, "but Mr. and Mrs. Stanton may be interested to know that a couple of the long-term foster parents will be returning to Sparrow Island from their vacation tomorrow. They've already agreed to take Moses this weekend, so he won't have to leave the island after all."

To Abby's surprise, her mother did not look the least bit upset about Moses' upcoming transfer to the other family. At first she thought that maybe the child's close call the other day had rattled her mother enough to make her want him to be with a younger and more experienced foster family. But the truth was that Ellen seemed more serene now than she had before the CPR incident. Abby couldn't explain the shift in her mother's attitude, but whatever the cause, she was glad that Ellen seemed to have found a new level of peace.

Having tired of trying to push Finnegan's floppy ears up under the cap, Beau turned to Joanne and began pulling on her arm again.

"Wan' go," he insisted.

"Okay, we're going," she said, bending to pick up the laundry bag she'd dropped earlier.

Apparently that wasn't quick enough for the toddler who was growing impatient. Letting his knees go rubbery beneath him, he dropped to the floor and reached for her to pick him up.

"Mama!"

Joanne wasn't much for kowtowing to a child's acting-out behaviors, but this time, her face softened and she knelt to wrap her arms around the boy. Mimicking her, he got up on his knees and put his arms around her neck.

"I'm not your mama," she said gently. "I'm Joanne."

He tried to parrot the word, but he had trouble forming the sound with his misshapen lip.

"I promise you, though. We're going to find you a mama."

Beau smiled and hugged her neck so tight she coughed.

"Find mama!" he declared.

AFTER TERZA FOLLOWED Joanne and Beau out, Henry walked over to where Ellen sat holding Moses on her lap. He bent and tickled the baby's chin. "Cute little guy," he said to no one in particular. Then he addressed the baby himself. "We're doing our best to find your folks, little buddy."

Mary had been watching her boyfriend and it was clear that she was touched by his sensitive behavior.

"Why don't you all relax while I get dinner started," Abby told the others. "Henry, can you stay and eat with us?"

"Thank you, but no, I'm still on duty," he said, checking his watch. "I can only stay a few minutes. Mary, would you like to go out on the porch for some fresh air?"

After they went outside, George followed Abby into the kitchen. "There are plenty of leftovers to heat up," he suggested as he helped her rummage through the refrigerator. "You and Mary should take some of these casseroles home with you."

As they puttered in the kitchen, Abby enjoyed the time alone with her father. As a child, she'd been a miniature shadow to the man who, in her eyes, knew everything. They had explored the woods together, finding and identifying various plants and creatures, and he had helped foster her love of birds. She still recalled with pleasure the time he had placed a long, wriggling earthworm in her small hand for inspection. When she hadn't flinched but merely leaned in to get a better look at its segmented body, he had proudly declared her to be "intrepid." That simple statement, even though she hadn't known exactly what it meant at the time, had made her feel very grownup and worthy in his eyes. And when he'd explained that the word meant bold and fearless, his proud acceptance made her want to explore more of the fascinating world that her father showed her.

Later, when Abby had learned about God in church, she imagined that He was like her flesh and blood father: A kind and patient teacher and guardian, full of encouragement and comfort. George was someone she could go to with any problem, no matter how great or small, and he would help her work her way through it. To her, God was just like that.

She opened a large container of chicken soup and decided that a salad and some crusty French bread would go nicely with that.

The phone on the wall rang, jerking her out of her thoughts. George reached for it and greeted the caller with a cheerful, "Good evening!"

As Abby poured the soup into the pot to heat, she watched his expression suddenly turn serious.

"Yes, he's still here, Joanne. Hold on a sec and I'll get him for you."

George dashed from the room and came back with Henry hot on his heels.

The sheriff took the phone and listened for a moment before asking, "How long has he been missing?"

By this time, Abby didn't even make a pretense of tending the dinner as she turned her back to the stove and blatantly eavesdropped on the conversation.

"Did you check inside the house?" He frowned and rubbed the top of his head. "What about the shed?"

Now Ellen and Mary drifted into the kitchen to see what was going on. Moses squirmed in his sling, apparently waking to the noise, activity and aromas in the kitchen.

"I'll be right there."

Henry hung up the phone and reached for the communications radio attached to his belt. After calling in a report of a missing toddler at the Flemming residence on Primrose Lane, he quickly described to the group in the kitchen what had happened.

"Joanne had helped him out of the car and was carrying some laundry and other things into the house. She thought he was right behind her, but after she set the stuff down on the back porch, she turned around and he was nowhere in sight."

Without further ado, Henry turned and ran outside, but he'd barely started the car when Abby rapped on his passenger window.

"Let me in. I'm going too!"

CHAPTER ❧ FOURTEEN

BUGS, SNAKES AND FEAR of the falling darkness. These were only a few of the dangers that lurked in the woods for Beau. More worrisome were possibilities of wild animals protecting their young or birds of prey taking an interest in the defenseless child.

But the most likely concerns were uneven terrain that sloped down to the sea at the farthest edge of the Flemmings' property. Given how long he'd been gone, Henry said he didn't think the boy would have walked that far afield. Not yet, anyway.

Keeping her eyes peeled to the ground ahead of her, Abby stayed in a straight line with the others walking through the woods. The searchers consisted of church members, volunteer firefighters and anyone who'd heard through the grapevine that a child was in trouble. Abby's throat was growing raw, but she shouted again for Beau. The boy's name rippled through the line of searchers as they called for him, over and over.

The first thing Henry and his deputies had done when they had arrived at the Flemming home was to conduct a thorough search of the house, car, shed and yard. Abby had hoped they'd find the child playing hide-and-seek in a closet as Henry said happens sometimes in cases of missing children, but the only thing they'd found was the plastic toy action figure he'd been playing with earlier. It had been dropped behind the yard, on a dirt trail that Clint Flemming used whenever he went fishing.

That prompted a hasty search of the area by deputies on the scene who ultimately turned up nothing. Henry had called for the search-and-rescue dogs from Orcas Island, but it would be a while before they arrived by boat.

Meanwhile, the weak rays of fading sunlight meant that the thermal imaging camera the deputies had brought with them was still mostly useless. That piece of equipment worked best in the dark, but Abby hoped that Beau would be found before then and they wouldn't have to use it.

It hadn't been long before Janet Heinz, Rev. Hale and his wife, and about twenty other church members showed up. Even Pete and Tamara, who had been meeting with the pastor when the call arrived, came along to lend their support.

"Mary called and asked me to activate the prayer chain," Janet explained. "I told her we could pray while we're searching."

Considering her dress and modest heels, the bubbly secretary was not exactly outfitted for a trek through the woods, but that didn't stop her from getting in there and running her hose or snagging her rayon dress on rough branches.

Likewise, Tamara wore a full-skirted, peach-colored short sleeved dress with a white lace collar. In her case, it wasn't the clothing that impeded her search efforts, but the fact that she was too out of shape to be marching up and down the vine-tangled hillside.

"Tamara was breathing so hard I was afraid she'd have a heart attack or something," Jenny said when Abby asked where the young woman had gone. "I suggested she go back to the house and keep Joanne company."

Pete hadn't returned to the yard with her. The couple had acted very stiff with each other, even more so than last Sunday, leading Abby to conclude that they'd been in a difficult counseling session with Rev. Hale when the call had come in. Abby had to hand it to the couple, though, for putting the welfare of this little boy ahead of their own problems.

Most of their search had taken place along the southern end of the wooded area behind the Flemming property since the northernmost part was carpeted with a thick, seemingly impenetrable, underbrush. "Kids usually take the path of least resistance," Henry had assured them.

Unfortunately, after more than an hour of calling and hoping that every odd-shaped sapling or fallen branch in the rapidly darkening dusk was Beau, the group returned empty handed and disheartened.

As they emerged from the forest, Abby peered into the yard, hoping against hope that Beau would be back at the house waiting to greet the volunteers with his funny lopsided grin. Instead, Mary, Finnegan and George waited in the yard with Joanne and Tamara for the group's return.

Despite the dropping temperature, Abby was hot and sweaty as she crossed the yard toward her father and sister. Mary handed her a paper towel from the tote bag affixed to her chair, and Abby used it to wipe her face and the nape of her neck.

Vince and Cheryl Emory made the rounds of the returning

searchers, offering bottled drinks and granola bars that had been left from Tuesday's walkathon and cookout.

Pete Preston walked past his wife without a word of acknowledgment and stood between Abby and Mary. His body language to his wife was clear: *These people are my buffer. Keep your distance.*

Abby wished there was something she could say or do that would help the situation. Help this couple reconnect. Tamara was a sweet young woman whose shyness made her a little hard to get to know. Although Abby's priorities were focused on finding Beau right now, later she would suggest that she and Ellen, and Mary if she was available, make a lunch date with her. The purpose would not be to pry into her marital difficulties, but just to let her know that she had friends in the church who cared about her.

As for Pete, Abby didn't have as clear a picture how to reach out to him.

Finnegan turned and looked up at the man who seemed so troubled. Pete stooped down, resting his weight on one heel, and patted the dog's head. It was amazing how, even when humans couldn't connect, a dog could always open the door.

"I want to go back and look for the boy," Pete said, "but the deputy says we've done all we can do for now."

Some of the deputies and firefighters, equipped with flashlights and communication radios, were still wandering the woods, but Henry had called the civilians out for fear that someone might get injured or lost out there.

After a moment, Mary spoke up. "Pete, we're going to find him. I know we will."

He didn't look away from the dog, and when he answered, it

was as though he was addressing Finnegan. "Just last Sunday Beau was turning around on the church pew, making funny faces at me and trying to get me to laugh. It was all I could do to keep from busting out in the middle of Rev. Hale's sermon."

Finnegan inched over toward him and rested his chin on Pete's knee.

They stayed like that for a long moment. Henry's announcement that the search dogs would arrive soon and that in the meantime he would be taking the thermal imaging camera into the woods to try to detect the heat of the child's body was of little encouragement to the searchers. Essentially, it just reinforced that their efforts had failed and that it wasn't going to be an easy matter to find Beau.

Mary took the dog's leash and handed it to Pete. "Here, take Finnegan. He's been wanting to help ever since we got here."

Abby had no doubt that the dog understood something very serious was going on. She just hoped this wouldn't be another futile search. At this point, however, just doing something—anything—gave the group renewed hope.

As Pete rounded up a fresh flashlight, a radio and a shirt of Beau's for Finnegan to sniff, Henry gently cautioned him not to get his hopes up too high. "Finnegan is plenty smart and he's a good service dog, but he's not trained for tracking."

Pete gave a stiff nod and headed off into the woods, the headlights from the patrol cars flooding the yard and a short distance into the woods. All eyes watched and all hearts prayed as the bystanders waited hopefully for the golden lab to lead Pete to the boy.

Along with the others, Abby watched until the pair was out of sight. She was aware that they were all straining to hear

Pete's feet crunching heavily on twigs or rustling through leaves. In the quiet, Finnegan's eager whines carried to them through the darkening night.

After a few minutes, those sounds were inaudible, drowned out by the chorus of night creatures and the restless movements of the people left behind.

Rev. Hale, his wife Patricia, and a few of the Flemmings' closest friends from church had formed what looked like a protective circle around the couple. Soon, they all held hands, their heads bowed, as the pastor led them in a quiet prayer.

Abby said one of her own, her gaze lifting to the star-speckled sky, and asked God to watch over the little boy and to lead Finnegan and Pete straight to him. Next to her, Mary folded her hands in her lap, and Abby knew that her sister was also pleading with God for the child's safety.

Finally, Janet could stand the uneasy silence no more.

"I wonder if it's possible Beau could have been kidnapped."

Cheryl Emory and Sandy McDonald simultaneously gasped at the suggestion. Another woman, someone Abby didn't know but had seen on occasion at The Green Grocer, scowled in response.

"You shouldn't even say such a thing," the woman chided, pushing her lanky brown hair behind her shoulder. "That's the way rumors get started."

Henry, having overheard the conversation, stepped closer to quell the tension.

"It's a reasonable question," he said, "and one that we've already considered." He squelched the handheld radio and gave a brief instruction to one of the other officers before continuing. "Considering the fact that the Flemming property is so far off the road, and that Clint had been home working in the yard just prior to his wife and the child returning home, it's not likely that anyone would have been lurking here on the off chance of committing such a crime."

Janet turned to the woman and briefly lifted her eyebrows. Any further dialogue about the matter was clipped when several among the group in the Flemmings' yard turned to stare toward the trail as Finnegan's quick, chuffing barks drifted to them. He was obviously excited about something. Abby offered up a prayer that it was a positive excitement that was causing the normally quiet dog to bark.

Her gaze followed the pointed fingers, and she stepped behind Mary's chair to move her so she could see her dog loop around a cluster of low bushes and then lead Pete deeper into the woods.

Brambles tore at Pete's stylish black slacks as he pushed through the thicket. The tall sandy-blond man hesitated only a moment, then ducked to avoid overhanging tree limbs as he followed the dog out of their line of sight.

A hush came over the group who only seconds before had been talking among themselves or calling others on their cell phones to give status reports. Abby prayed fervently that Finnegan had detected Beau's scent or heard the child's cry.

Mary reached up and slipped her fingers into Abby's hand, and the two women prayed out loud, beseeching God to lead the pair straight to Beau. A happy, healthy Beau.

Henry shook his head as dog and man disappeared from sight. "I just hope they're not following a rabbit."

DURING THE NEXT twenty torturous minutes Henry gave directions to the dog team that had docked at the marina, and communications radios squawked from a dozen or more places throughout the crowd.

By now, every time a voice rattled over any of the radios, Abby found herself instantly on alert to hear what was being said. Until now, Pete had answered Henry's questions with disappointing reports that they'd found nothing. But this transmission was different.

"We need your prayers," Pete's electronic voice blared at them.

Abby's heart clutched and Joanne gasped. Clint put his arm around his wife, and Rev. Hale moved closer to the couple. Abby wasn't sure, but she thought she heard a high-pitched voice mingled with Pete's.

"But this time, make 'em prayers of thanks," Pete added. "Say hi, little buddy."

And then the sweetest words, spoken in an adorably child-ish way, came through the radio waves. "Wha's 'at?"

There was a click followed by a loud squelch.

Joanne turned to her husband and finally, after holding her composure throughout this whole ordeal, wept as though her heart would burst from the sheer joy of knowing that her foster son was alive. While Clint held her close, Jenny moved nearer and patted her back while murmuring soothing words.

Pete keyed the mike again and this time he was laughing. "Beau's going to be an electrical engineer when he grows up. He wants to try all the buttons on the radio to see how it works."

The joke was exactly what the group in the yard needed . . . an opportunity to release the long-held tension through laugh-ter. Wild, crazy, delirious laughter, accompanied by high-fives, hugs and even spontaneous jigs of joy.

A couple of minutes later, Finnegan led the way into the

clearing, looking over his shoulder at man and child to make sure they were following him.

The dog continued dancing around Pete's legs as the people in the yard mobbed them. Beau looked tired but alert. Mingled among the excited voices were Finnegan's happy little chuffing barks, announcing to the world that all was now well again.

A camera flashed, capturing the picture of an ecstatic rescuer with a bewildered toddler clinging to his neck. Abby expected that William Jansen, *The Birdcall's* editor-in-chief, would run it on the front page of next week's paper.

She waited with Mary and George while the others surrounded the trio and was amused to see Jenny pushing through the throng of well-wishers to clear a path for Joanne and Clint.

Once Beau was reunited with his foster parents and whisked into the house to be examined by paramedics, Pete described how they'd found him.

"If it hadn't been for Finnegan, I would have walked right on by," he said, reaching down to give the dog a congratulatory rub. "Beau was curled up beside a fallen tree branch, snoozing for all he was worth. I had just stepped over the branch and was about to keep on going when Finnegan pulled on his leash and started barking at a lump on the ground."

If Henry wasn't inside with the foster family, Abby would have ribbed him for doubting the dog's tracking abilities, specially trained or not.

"If he hadn't been there," Pete continued, "I would have thought it was just a clump of leaves on the ground next to the branch. It was really hard to see, even with the flashlight, but I'm glad we got him back safe and sound."

After a few prodding questions from William Jansen, they

learned that Beau had actually walked pretty far off the foot-path and into an area dense with underbrush. It was anyone's guess how he had managed to go that far before falling asleep.

On the outskirts of the excited group of onlookers, Tamara stood by, waiting patiently to rejoin her husband. When she made no move to go to Pete's side, Abby realized she may have worried that he would respond with the same frostiness he had exhibited earlier.

Now that they knew Beau was all right, the crowd began to disperse. George asked Abby and Mary to wait while he went inside to see if the Flemmings needed anything, so Abby sat on the steps leading to the back porch. Mary was making a fuss over Finnegan, telling him what a smart, heroic dog he was.

Rev. Hale walked by Pete and laid a hand on his shoulder. "Congratulations. That was nice work." Although he lowered his voice, it carried across the yard that was now quiet except for tree toads and crickets. "Are you and Tamara going to be all right?"

Tamara still hadn't approached her husband and she seemed anxious to hear his answer.

Pete thought about what the preacher had asked and ran a hand through his hair. Finally, he said, "Yes, this whole experience has made me see things differently."

The pastor shook his hand. "Good, I'm glad to hear it. Call me if you need me. You have my number at home."

Pete nodded, and as Rev. Hale left to round up Patricia from inside the house, he moved toward his wife, holding out a hand toward her.

For a moment, it looked as though Tamara wasn't sure what he wanted, but when she realized that his gesture was concilia-tory, she teared up and ran into his arms.

The two stood like that a long time, Pete kissing the top of her head and both of them apologizing to each other.

Abby looked at Mary to suggest they head toward the van so that the couple could have some privacy, but Mary shook her head.

"Let's not disturb them," Mary said quietly. "Right now the best thing they can do is finish saying what's in their hearts."

To turn her attention away from the couple, Abby put her arms around Finnegan's neck and told him that his picture would show up in next week's newspaper. The canine sat like a soldier beside Mary's chair, but there was no mistaking the big doggy grin he gave her.

The Prestons took their conversation to the bench on the other side of the shrub from Abby.

"I'm sorry for being so angry with you," Pete said. "It was all my fault. I should have been at home with you instead of chasing after the almighty dollar. Rev. Hale was right. I've been valuing worldly success over godly success. Going after that promotion and the number-one sales position like it was the be-all and end-all of the universe."

Tamara murmured something about being the one at fault, but he cut her off.

"We've both done things we're not proud of," he said. "Mine was stepping over the line to steal that big account from the other salesman, but it didn't make me feel good. It only made me feel like dirt."

Abby squirmed, thinking it was long past time to go, but it would be even more embarrassing to get up now and let them know she and Mary had heard everything he said.

"You're my family," he said, "and without my family I'm as lost as little Beau was out there in the woods."

They grew silent for a moment and Abby imagined that they were holding each other. At least, that's what she hoped was happening. It would be so much nicer than the way they'd been with each other for the past week or so.

When Pete spoke again, his words were husky with regret. "I hope you can forgive me for neglecting you."

Tamara's voice was soft in response. "Yes, if you can find it in your heart to forgive me for—"

"It's over," Pete cut in. "All is forgiven. The next step is to forget. I'm willing to try. How about you?"

CHAPTER ❀ FIFTEEN

Just as I suspected, the cousins Warren and Conrad recanted their rare bird sightings when I asked them to come to my office to notify the birding society."

Abby shifted her position on her parents' sofa to better accommodate the squirming bundle in her arms and smiled when Moses arched his body for a full-length stretch and yawn.

"They admitted they've been competitive with each other all their lives and this was just another way to try to outdo the other."

After the ordeal with Beau the night before, Abby and Mary had headed home and told their father that they would stop by on Friday evening for the dinner they had missed out on. It was especially meaningful to be with their parents tonight since this was the final night that Moses would spend with Ellen and George.

"So your class is over now, eh?" George asked. "How did that experiment go?"

Abby smiled at the word *experiment*. She sometimes taught an accredited course on wildlife biology to college students from nearby University of Washington. At other times, she took schoolchildren on field trips. And the outings for tourists generally ranged from an hour or two covering the basics of San Juan birdlife to an all-day or two- to three-day event. This time, in response to requests from birders who wanted more than the basic beginner offerings, Abby had developed a ten-day course for serious bird-watching hobbyists.

"It was a lot of fun. They had a lot more in-depth questions than I usually get, so it was an interesting challenge for me." Abby made a face at Moses who seemed not to notice. So she entertained them both by letting him grasp her pinky fingers and gently bouncing his arms up and down. "I'm not sure if we'll do it again. It depends on whether enough advanced birders sign up for it. So my last day with this group was bittersweet. It's nice to have the work behind me, but I'm going to miss the individuals that I've come to know and enjoy."

She was thinking especially of the older sisters who were willing to do anything she asked, and who never once complained about the heat or the mosquitoes.

Elaine and Delphine's relationship with each other was clearly based on a concern for the other that surpassed their own personal interests. They'd even extended that concern to other members of the group, sometimes sacrificing an opportunity for a stupendous photograph so that they could alert the others to the bird's fleeting appearance. The sisters were so caring and giving that it was a joy to be around them.

The same couldn't be said of Warren and Conrad whose relationship, though affectionate, was nothing like the healthy, collegial camaraderie that existed between Elaine and Delphine.

And though Jenny and Charlotte had begun to soften toward each other, thanks to some gentle coaxing and encouragement from the sisters, they still had a long way to go to build the kind of generous-spirited friendship that was possible if they'd only set aside their own selfish concerns long enough to consider the other's feelings.

"I know what you mean," Ellen said. "It's going to be sad when Moses goes to his long-term foster family tomorrow, but it's time for him to have a place to settle in."

As a unit, Abby, Mary and George all turned to see how she felt about the upcoming transfer. Before coming here tonight, the sisters had speculated about their mother's state of mind after becoming so attached to the baby, but Abby was relieved to see that she seemed to be handling it very well.

George gave Ellen a private smile that seemed like a cross between a morale booster and a reminder of an earlier conversation in which they had already covered this territory.

"Your dad's going to be busy catching up with his farm work tomorrow," Ellen continued, "so I was wondering if one of you girls would mind giving me a lift to the Senior Center. The day that Moses turned up, I left my bag of cookbooks and recipes. I'm sure no one has taken anything from it, but I want to get it back before it's put away where I won't be able to find it later."

Mary reached into her bag and gave Finnegan a milk bone treat. "I promised Candace I'd come in tomorrow and make up some new flower arrangements, but that can wait until Monday."

Abby knew what a sacrifice that would be for Mary's shop since most of her walk-in sales were from weekend tourists. "There's no need for you to do that," she said. "I have the whole day tomorrow with nothing planned, so that would be a great opportunity for Mom and me to spend some quality time together."

Mary smiled her thanks, then turned to their mother. "And you and I can have our quality time next week." She held out her arms to Abby. "It's my turn to hold Moses now."

Abby got up and carried the baby to her sister. With a baby of this age, there was only so much a person could do to entertain it. Besides, she supposed he could only take so much arm bouncing.

"Sam and I saw Clint Flemming today while we were repairing the fence that separates our properties." George got up to retrieve a pacifier from the bassinet and handed it to Mary. "Apparently Beau took off into the woods yesterday because he misunderstood what Joanne had told him about finding a mother for him. It seems he thought his mother was *lost* and that he needed to go and look for her."

Mary took the pacifier through a make-believe airplane flight before sliding it into the baby's mouth. "Leave it to a three-year-old to make that kind of mistake. It reminds me of the time Dad was leaving the house to help a friend with a personal matter. When we asked him where he was going, he said 'to see a man about a horse,' which was his way of telling us it was none of our business. Well, Abby got all excited and couldn't understand why Dad drove his car home instead of riding the horse."

Abby laughed. "It was the summer between first grade and second. I must have bugged you about that horse for days."

"Weeks," George corrected. "Anyway, Clint has decided to put up a fence around his backyard. Joanne had thought they didn't need one since she only lets the kids outside when she's with them, but Beau's little adventure changed her mind about that."

Ellen had been fairly quiet, and it occurred to Abby that she must have asked for a ride to the Senior Center to distract herself from the empty house after the social worker left with the baby tomorrow.

"Mom, are you okay about Moses leaving?"

Ellen drew a deep breath and let it out slowly before responding. "I'm going to miss him, no doubt about that, but the important thing is that he's accomplished what the Lord sent him here to do."

Confused, Abby looked to Mary who seemed just as baffled by their mother's comment as she was.

"Moses was born on July 9," she explained. "That was the same date your brother died fifty-seven years ago."

Abby slipped off her shoes and crossed her legs on the sofa. Realization dawned slowly. Now things were starting to make sense.

Though Mary was too young to remember him and Abby had come along a couple of years after he'd passed away, she and Mary had been told they had a brother and that he'd died as an infant. Their parents hadn't gone into any specifics and, being sensitive children who understood that the subject caused their parents pain, they hadn't pressed for any more information. They never knew his name.

"George David Stanton Jr., was only two months old when it happened." Ellen got up and poured herself another cup of tea from the teapot on the coffee table. When she set the pot back down, she let her finger trace the new dent on the spout. "Mary was just a little over a year old at the time, so I had my hands full taking care of two babies. After lunch I put Davy down for a nap. He never woke up."

Ellen returned to her chair and stirred the sugar into her tea as she stirred up the old memory.

"At the time, doctors called it crib death," George filled in while she sipped her tea. "Nowadays, they refer to it as SIDS. Sudden Infant Death Syndrome."

Abby watched her mother staring down into her cup and wondered if she was remembering or praying.

"I always wondered if there was something I could have done to prevent it from happening, she finally said, rousing herself from her thoughts. "Then every summer, the anniversary of Davy's death rolled around and brought it all back."

George set down the remote control device he'd been toying with and met Abby's gaze directly. When, as a teenager, she'd asked about their mother's recurring solemn mood, he had told her and Mary to be patient. Ellen would talk about it when she was ready. It had taken fifty-seven years, and Abby was glad her mother had finally found the strength to bring up the sad event and discuss it openly.

Mary moved the baby to the crook of her arm. "But the rest of the time you were always so happy, like nothing bothered you. I thought you had managed to move on. You had so much of what you called 'joy in the Lord.'"

Cradling the cup in her hand, Ellen traced the elegant floral pattern with one thumb. "People can have joy in the Lord even when their lives aren't perfect. We did move on," she said, glancing toward George, "but losing a child is something that never completely goes away. Especially when there are unanswered questions about his death.

"When Terza and I brought Moses back, he got a second

chance and so did we." She gazed up at George, seemingly drawing strength from the connection she found there. "And, in a way, Moses brought me the answer I've been needing for so long. I believe God used Moses' emergency the other day to give me the chance to spare someone else's child."

She got up again and crossed to where Mary sat holding the baby. When Mary lifted him up for their mother to take, Ellen hugged him to her chest and briefly closed her eyes as she touched her cheek to his head.

"I wanted to tell you this," she said addressing Abby and Mary, "so that you'll know you don't have to worry about me. I'm ready to move on and use my experience to help others."

Ellen stroked the baby's cheek and smiled as he puckered his lips and turned toward her hand.

"And now Moses is ready to move on and bless someone else's life."

ELLEN HAD INSISTED that she didn't need Abby there when the social worker arrived to take Moses to his new family who would keep him until either his birth parents claimed him or he was adopted. Despite her mother's protestations that she and George would be fine with the transfer, Abby was glad that she had insisted on coming over anyway.

Moses' piles of knitted goodies and the rest of his clothes, diapers, toys and formula had already been stacked in a cardboard box and set by the front door. The bassinet was on loan from the Flemmings, and George had thoughtfully returned it this morning so that Ellen wouldn't have to look at the empty bed after Moses was gone.

Abby lifted the box and carried it out to the caseworker's car so her parents could focus on saying their good-byes to the baby. When she returned, Ellen was tearfully handing Moses to the sweet young woman who was trying her best to make this as painless as possible.

"I'm not allowed to tell you the name of his new foster parents," she said with a smile, "but I expect this won't be the last you'll see of Moses. It's a small island after all."

After Abby and her parents watched the car leave their driveway with its precious cargo securely fastened into an infant seat, she gave them both a hug.

"I'm sorry we weren't able to find his birth parents," Abby said. "Even if he ends up being adopted, it would be nice to know who they are for his medical records."

"It's okay," Ellen said, laying a hand on her arm. "We don't always need to know all the answers. God will take care of the necessary details."

Ellen didn't want to hang around the farm after that, for which Abby couldn't blame her. While George went out to the barn to take care of some neglected chores, Abby drove Ellen to the Senior Center in what was turning out to be a full-circle visit.

Once there, she parked by the curb and both of them got out, examining the surroundings as if they half expected to see the baby's mother crouching in the bushes.

A curtain moved at the window and the door opened a moment later. Tamara stepped out, looking happier than Abby had ever seen her.

"I thought that was you." The young blonde stepped back to let them in, then gave Ellen a welcoming hug. "We've missed you here at the Senior Center."

Tamara definitely appeared more rested than she had at the

Flemmings' house the other night. Today she wore a blue-and-yellow floral sundress with pockets on the front. A flap of white lace folded over the pocket and hooked over a button in the shape of a flower. Abby noted that, although pockets often made heavy people look larger, Tamara actually looked a little slimmer today.

"It's good to see you again," Abby said as they moved into the activity room where Emma Stoltz, Mr. Phillips and some others were tying fly-fishing lures. "That dress really looks good on you."

"She made it herself," Emma bragged. "That lace on the pockets was my idea. She wasn't going to do it, but I think if a person has a certain skill, it should be their trademark, you know?"

Tamara's shyness apparently kicked in, making her uncomfortable with the unsolicited attention. "Brenda Wilson is here from The Tackle Shop, showing us how to make fishing flies. Would you like to join us?" As if anticipating their hesitation, she added, "They make great Christmas gifts for the fishermen and women in your life."

Abby wouldn't mind sticking around if that was what her mother wanted to do, but Ellen turned away and scanned the room.

"Thanks, but we just popped in to pick up the tote bag of cookbooks and recipe supplies that I left here a couple of weeks ago."

Tamara's frown made it clear that she hadn't seen the tote bag.

"It's over here," Emma said, rising from the cluttered activity table. She led them past open tubs of sewing notions.

Abby peeked into the one filled with ribbons of all sorts and wasn't surprised to find a large spool of the pale blue ribbon from In Stitches. After all, Ana Dominguez had said she sold lots of that particular style for sewing and craftwork. And Abby couldn't think of a single place on the island that saw more craftwork than these four walls. Above the shelf that held the tubs was a hand-lettered sign proclaiming, DONATE YOUR UNWANTED MAGAZINES HERE.

She paused and stared up at the sign, studying the squared off letters. The topmost line of the thick black O's sagged slightly as if they were tired of holding up their own weight.

"Oh, look at these," Ellen exclaimed as she sorted through a box of dog-eared ladies' magazines. Her own over-laden bag sat at her feet. "Someone must have donated some new ones."

Abby gave herself a mental shake. *Don't be ridiculous. Lots of people print in block letters when they make large signs*, she reminded herself. *Besides, how many of these elderly folks were likely to have given birth lately?* This obsession with finding Moses' mother was really getting to her.

Abby sidled up next to Ellen, pleased at the enthusiasm with which she flipped through the magazines, looking for new recipes. "Take your time," she urged. "I have all day."

"Here's a recipe for green bean casserole with raisins, peaches and onions." Ellen shoved an open magazine into her hand and jabbed a finger at the page. Someone had drawn a star beside the recipe and written *Yummy!* "Doesn't that look interesting?"

Actually, it looked disgusting, but Abby wasn't about to say that when the person who'd jotted the comment could very easily be one of the people hunched over the table nearby, tying feathers to fishing barbs.

Then she saw the sparkle in her mother's widened eyes, an expression of mischief that was held firmly suppressed behind tightened lips that dared not smile.

And Abby remembered. All those potluck suppers at church when she was a child . . . full of textures and tastes and colors that adults love but that make kids queasy. She'd been required, for politeness' sake, to occasionally try a small spoonful of something that one of her parents' friends was especially proud of. Usually creamed something-or-other that set her gag reflexes into overdrive. The worst part was that they always asked, "How do you like it?"

Abby didn't get into trouble for her honesty the first time she answered that question, but her parents had taken no chances after that. Subsequent potluck dinners were approached with extensive coaching. "You don't have to say it's terrible," her mother had said. "Just tell them it's *interesting.* That way, you can be honest without hurting anyone's feelings."

She hugged her mother, thanking God for giving her parents with a sense of humor.

"Yes, it's interesting. Very creative, in fact," she said, embellishing their old standby comment.

Ellen blew her an air kiss and continued searching through the magazines.

It looked like they might be here awhile, so Abby idly flipped through the magazine. She skipped past the parenting and home decorating articles and stopped at a photograph of a triangular birdhouse that could be affixed to the side of a tree or an upright post on a porch. This looked simple enough that she could use it as a project for schoolchildren visiting the conservatory, or maybe even to teach to the scouts in the Skills and Crafts group at church.

"Do you suppose it would be all right if I borrow this?" she asked her mother.

Emma set down the magazine she was looking at and answered for her. "Anything that's over six months old is fair game," she told her. "That one's been around since Mr. Phillips led a birdhouse-building group here at the center. So help yourself."

Abby thanked her and tucked the magazine in her mother's tote bag and looped the straps over her shoulder.

Ellen indicated she was ready to go, so they said their good-byes and headed toward the door. As they passed by the kitchen, Tamara popped out and waved a dish towel at them, saying she was looking forward to seeing Ellen later this week. Then she returned to her work in the kitchen.

Remembering her desire to show Tamara that a loving church family awaited her at Little Flock, Abby stopped her mother with a hand to her elbow. "Didn't you say Tamara has only lived here a couple of years and that she doesn't have many friends her age?"

Ellen nodded. "She keeps to herself a lot when she's not volunteering at the Senior Center. I told her I wanted to introduce her to Ida Tolliver, but it's never quite worked out."

"Maybe it's hard for her to meet people in groups," Abby said, thinking of some of her dearest friends over the years who'd been far from the life of the party. "Why don't we invite her over for a Stanton family dinner after church tomorrow? She already knows us, and even if she gets a little overwhelmed, Finnegan will know how to put her at ease."

"That's a wonderful idea!"

That was all the prompting Ellen needed, so Abby followed

her into the kitchen where they found Tamara sitting on a stool, wiping the counter clear of the snacks that had been served earlier.

She started at their entry, looking for all she was worth like she'd been caught with her hand in the cookie jar. She giggled nervously.

"I was just trying to rest my feet," she said. "My ankles sometimes get swollen when I'm on my feet too much."

"Honey, you should put your feet up any chance you get," Ellen said. Quickly, she launched into her dinner invitation and even asked Tamara her favorite dish so she could prepare it for her.

"Thank you. I wish I could come," she said regretfully, "but Pete will be leaving a little after noon tomorrow for a few days on the mainland. I'd like to spend that time with him before he has to go."

"Of course, dear." Ellen patted her shoulder and turned to go. "Your husband is definitely a priority. Perhaps we can do it some other time. Of course, we'd want you to bring Pete as well."

Shy or not, Tamara seemed sincerely disappointed at having to turn down their invitation, which gave Abby confidence that she would, indeed, join them at a future time.

She slid off her stool and followed Ellen to the door. "I know! Why don't you come over to my place afterward for dessert?" She motioned toward Abby. "You too, of course. I'd love to have some company."

Ellen smiled first at Abby, then took Tamara's hand and patted it. "That's a lovely idea. And it will be nice to get out and socialize after tending to the baby these past two weeks."

THE PRESTONS DIDN'T SHOW UP for church the next day. Abby assumed that Pete's early afternoon departure had kept them home packing and getting in some quality time before he was to take off for his next weeks-long absence. Even so, she wished the couple could have joined them for Ellen's delicious meatloaf dinner. But the important thing was that they would have time to visit with Tamara in another hour or so.

For now, the Stantons, as well as Bobby and his parents, were relaxing out back, their bellies full. While the other adults sat on the porch and talked, Abby and Bobby had gone out into the yard to play a modified version of Frisbee with Finnegan who was enjoying his exercise for the day. The huckleberry and rose bushes at the edge of the yard defined their boundaries.

Mary pushed her chair forward on the deck and spoke a little louder so that everyone, including Abby, could hear her. "Bobby can we see your trophy and certificate from the walkathon?"

Although the walkathon had taken place on Tuesday, the Skills and Crafts leaders had waited until today to present the awards in order to give the children time to collect the sponsor pledges. More importantly, they felt it necessary to recognize the young ones' efforts in front of the entire church and let everyone know the positive impact these kids were making far beyond their own church walls.

Abby grabbed the weighted cloth disk and pretended to throw it for Finnegan. He was on to her and didn't fall for that trick. So she tossed it to Bobby instead, but the dog intercepted it and took it to the porch with him to sit and pant in the shade. "I'd love to see them, Bobby."

Since one of the awards had been promised to the child with the most sponsors, Bobby had cleverly taken each pledge and broken it into the total number of people in the family. Apparently, his guilt about the duplicity had been weighing on his mind, which was why he had confessed to Abby about it the day of the walkathon. She'd advised him to revise the list of sponsors so that it was exactly as he'd received them. As it turned out, he had stormed that contest without even using the loophole.

Bobby nodded and sat down on the step near her and mumbled to Abby, "I gave the prizes away."

Sandy McDonald leaned forward and beamed at her son. "I'm proud of his accomplishments, but even prouder of what he did after he won the prizes." She paused until she had everyone's full attention. "He *donated* them to our sister church's Skills and Crafts group that we were raising the money for."

Abby playfully pinched his knee to let him know she supported his decision.

"I kept the trophy, though," he said.

Sandy urged him to show it to the group, so he ran to the car and returned with a foot-tall plastic trophy and a certificate. He handed them to Abby for her to look at and then pass around to the others.

On the trophy was a gold metallic plaque that shortened and paraphrased Proverbs 10:9: *The person of integrity walks securely.*

She passed it to her mother and then smoothed the certificate on her lap.

"I'm going to frame that," Bobby said, "and the trophy will remind me to always stay on God's path."

Mary had told Abby that Tamara had volunteered to make up the certificates for the walkathon as a way to get more involved in the church, and she had done a lovely job.

Printed on plain, cream-colored paper, the computer-generated image showed a scalloped border with an open lace design. The official wording on the certificate had been done in a tasteful italic font and the typesetter had chosen a large block style for Bobby's name.

Abby adjusted her glasses to stare at the words BOBBY McDONALD and was immediately taken with a sensation of familiarity and difference. The *O*'s in his name were in four straight lines, as if they'd been created with a miniature ruler. Immediately, an image came to mind of the saggy-topped *O* in the hand-lettered sign at the Senior Center.

Even the lace art on the certificate pushed a button in her memory. On this paper, the open parts of the lace graphic were clustered in groups of four, like the leaves of a dogwood blossom, but the image in Abby's mind involved clusters of three carefully stitched lace openings. It seemed like the puzzle pieces were finally coming together for Abby.

She handed the paper to her mother who was still examining the trophy and rose to her feet.

"Mom, we need to go see Tamara. Now."

"But it's too early, dear," she said as she studied the certificate that had just been passed to her. "She's not expecting us until two-thirty."

Abby gently took the items from her and handed them to George. Then, taking her mother's hand, she urged her to her feet.

"This can't wait. I'll explain on the way."

CHAPTER ❦ SIXTEEN

Tamara's eyes were red when she opened the door to Abby and Ellen. Now that she and Pete seemed to be on better terms, Abby supposed it must have been particularly hard to say good-bye for this latest trip.

The young woman spoke to them through the screen door, making no effort to open it. "*Um*, I'm sorry, I didn't—"

"We know we're early for dessert," Ellen said, pulling open the outer door and stepping inside as if Tamara had given her a red carpet welcome, "but there's something very important we need to talk to you about."

"Oh, *um*, please . . . come on in." She waited for Abby to step in front of her, then followed her in. "Have a seat any-where," she said, motioning toward the plush sofa and wing-back chair in the living room. "That chair by the fireplace is best if you have a bad back."

Ellen took the chair and Abby prowled the room, taking in the tasteful cherry wood furnishings and gold upholstery accented with red pillows. Homemade beige curtains hung from the windows, tied back by lacy-edged strips of fabric, and a deep red Persian rug brought all the colors in the room together.

"Nice place for an indoor picnic," Abby said, watching for Tamara's reaction.

She seemed to be at once surprised and relieved by Abby's statement, as if she had been anticipating this moment but hadn't expected it so soon. Tamara paced the room, looking occasionally toward the hallway. Clearing her throat, she pushed a blonde tendril behind her ear.

"We're not going to judge you, Tamara. We came to help," Ellen said, her tone both soothing and firm. "You need to be honest, though. You can only sweep stuff under the carpet for so long before you end up tripping over it."

Tamara sat down on the sofa and rested her forehead on her hands.

Abby quit her pacing and sat beside her. "Moses is your child," she said, cutting right to the heart of the matter. "A child by another man. And you couldn't pretend the baby was Pete's because if he did the math, he'd realize it happened when he was out of town. Isn't that right?"

Tamara nodded but didn't say anything.

"Because you're heavy, you were able to hide the pregnancy," Abby continued gently. "The hard part was figuring out how to tell Pete, and the longer you waited, the harder it was to tell him."

"That's right." As Tamara lifted her head, she wiped her eyes with the heels of her hands. "I didn't want Pete to know what a horrible thing I'd done," she said softly. "I didn't want to hurt him, but it turns out that I've hurt him a lot more by not being truthful right from the start. It's just that . . ." Her voice drifted off as she considered how to explain her actions.

At that moment, the doorway to the hall filled with Pete's tall frame. "It's just that I've been gone so much that Tamara didn't have much of an opportunity to tell me," he said, finishing for her. "And even when I was here, I wasn't very available."

He crossed the room and sat on the other side of his wife, putting an arm around her shoulder.

Ellen sat forward on the edge of her chair. "We're sorry for intruding. We thought you had gone to the mainland for a business trip."

Tamara quickly explained. "Pete and I have been talking all night. He already knew part of the story, but it was only last night that I told him about Moses. He canceled his trip so that we could get this straightened out."

"Things had gone way off course," Pete said, his voice hoarse, "but we're going to set it right. With each other, with the baby and with the town. We've already made a small start, thanks to Rev. Hale."

Tamara sniffed loudly. "For the past few weeks, the pastor has been working with us on our problems. "It started out with us going to him to get help communicating with each other. And last week, I finally got up the nerve to tell them both about the . . ." She hesitated as if trying to find a gentler way to say it, but finally just blurted it out. ". . . the affair."

Tamara turned and looked at her husband as she spoke.

"At first Pete got very angry, as he had every right to be. I thought for sure we'd end up getting a divorce."

He reached for her hand and laced their fingers together. "Rev. Hale made me see that I was partly to blame. I hadn't been loving my wife sacrificially, as the Bible instructs. Instead, I was totally focused on my career and making it to the top rung of the promotion ladder. I was gone all the time." He turned away from her and directed his comment to Ellen. "She got lonely, which is understandable."

Ellen stood and crossed the room to join them on the sofa. "Honey, if only you had told any of the people at the Senior Center, we could have helped you. We all love you and we would have put you in touch with Rev. Hale much sooner."

"You're right," Tamara said, "If I felt like I couldn't talk to Pete about it, I should have confided in a friend as soon as I knew I was expecting. But regardless of all that, I was responsible for being vulnerable to temptation," Tamara was quick to add. "During our two years on Sparrow Island, I expected Pete to fill all my needs for companionship and I hadn't made any attempts to cultivate friendships outside of the Senior Center. And even there, I just came, did my volunteer work, and went home. I shouldn't have expected Pete—or any other man—to fill that role."

"That's true," Ellen said. "Even in the best of marriages, a woman needs girlfriends with whom she can relate in a way that men and women can't. God designed us that way and He wants us to have friends."

"If I'd done that," Tamara said, "I would have been less likely to have my head turned because of loneliness."

Awkwardly, and with much hesitation, she explained she'd been feeling unloved and unworthy because her husband had been gone so much. And when he was home, he was so tired from traveling that all he wanted was to relax and watch television or putter on the computer. His sales job offered him lots of opportunities to be around people all day, so when he came home, he welcomed the chance to spend some time by himself. And self absorbed as he was, he hadn't noticed that his wife was unhappy and feeling ignored.

Shortly after he left for yet another trip last fall, this one longer than usual because he attended a training conference and then made the rounds of his customers, Tamara fell into the snare.

To entertain herself while Pete was gone, Tamara had attended the Flashback Festival alone. While she was distracting herself from her loneliness with hot dogs and ice cream, a rather attractive man—someone she recognized as being lonely, too—started up a conversation with her.

As she spoke, Abby could see how a little bit of flattery and attention would have felt like a glass of cool water to someone in the desert.

Tamara had already been a little "curvy," as she put it, when she and Pete had moved to Sparrow Island, and she had steadily put on weight ever since. The extra pounds, combined with her inability to make an emotional connection with her husband, had left her feeling ugly and undesirable. So naturally, when this guy Mike put some moves on her, she was like a fish being reeled in for dinner.

"I never intended for it to go that far," she was quick to explain. "I considered him as just a friend. Someone nice to talk to while we visited the attractions at the Flashback Festival. After a few days of just hanging around together and having fun, he invited me to have dinner with him at The Dorset."

She paused when Pete slumped and rubbed his hands through his hair.

Abby had done her share of dating and had had male friends over the years. Experience had taught her that some men have an ulterior motive, no matter how platonic they consider the friendship to be.

"You're young and idealistic," she told Tamara. "That's one

of the things that everyone at the Senior Center loves about you. Unfortunately, some people try to take advantage of people with that kind of personality."

"And that's exactly what happened," Tamara concurred. "I knew that nothing was happening between us and would have even introduced him to Pete if he'd been here, but I thought it wouldn't look right to be seen having dinner with a man who wasn't my husband. So I suggested that he come here, thinking that we would just eat a meal and maybe play some Scrabble. But he must have got the wrong idea because he showed up with a picnic basket and a steak dinner from the Springhouse Café. I started to spread the food out on the table, but he suggested we eat in the living room, in front of the fireplace . . ."

Abby finished it for her. "And temptation and opportunity collided."

Tamara laid a hand on Pete's knee as if to apologize for his having to hear this all over again.

"I was immediately ashamed of what I'd done and I asked Mike to leave. His vacation was scheduled to last a few more days, so I was prepared to avoid him for the rest of the time that he was here on the island." She tightened her jaw. "I never saw him again and I have no idea how to get in touch with him to tell him about Moses."

Abby sighed as she remembered that Mary told her Henry had made no progress with finding the man who'd stayed at The Dorset. With no city or state in which to begin looking, the chances of finding a Michael Johnson—if that was even his real name—were nil, so the sheriff's department had given up on that search.

On one hand that was a shame, because the man should be told that he'd fathered a child. But on the other hand, the blessing was that it would be less complicated without him in the picture if Tamara and Pete should raise Moses themselves.

"Then, nine months later, when Moses was about to be born, I gathered up the things that Mike had left at the house," Tamara continued. "Things I'd hidden from Pete . . . the picnic basket, the beach blanket, and the handkerchief. In a way, I thought that by getting rid of those things along with giving Moses away, I could pretend that night in early October had never happened.

"As it turned out, the baby's timing was perfect. He was born on Sunday evening. Since Ellen is so conscientious about being prepared when she's leading a crafting session, I knew she would be the first to arrive at the Senior Center. And I knew she would make sure he was well taken care of." Tamara's smile was bittersweet. "I watched from the First Baptist Church across the street until you and Abby put Moses in the car with you and drove away together."

Ellen looked thoughtful. "Giving birth is hard, even with medical help. How did you know what to do?"

Tamara scratched her arm distractedly. "My mother's best friend was a midwife. She was always telling stories about her work, including all of the less-than-delicate details. They talked very openly because they didn't know I was eavesdropping from the stairway." She paused, apparently remembering how she'd applied the information she'd learned over the years. "So when Moses was born, I just did the stuff the midwife had talked about."

"What are you going to do now?" Abby asked. "Whatever you decide, there are people at Little Flock Church who will still be your friend and who will help share both your burdens and your joys. We're your church family."

Tamara's tears resumed as she hugged Abby. With her free hand, she reached for Ellen who moved in for a group hug. When she pulled away, she lifted the hem of her dress to wipe the moisture from her eyes.

"We talked about that," she said, looking to her husband.

He reached up and tenderly brushed away a lingering tear from her cheek. "At first all I thought about was myself and how angry I was. But after I got over the shock of hearing that my wife had been pregnant and given birth without my knowing it, I thought about how Beau must have felt when he was lost and wandering in the woods as he looked for his mother. And then I began thinking that, if we didn't do something, Moses would have to live his whole life wondering what had happened to his mother."

He rubbed his hand along his jaw and the unshaved growth made a sound like sandpaper.

"When I found Beau sleeping beside that branch, I felt so much love for that little boy. Well, if I could feel that strongly about a kid I barely knew," he said, "then I know I can love and care for my wife's child, even if he doesn't share my blood. As you mentioned," he said, leaning past his wife to look at Abby, "We're all a part of the family of God."

Reaching into her purse, Abby pulled out her cell phone and opened the contact list to Henry's number. "You need to tell the sheriff everything you've told us."

"What she needs to do," Ellen interjected, "is see a doctor if she hasn't already. Make sure there aren't any medical problems as a result of giving birth by herself."

"I'm sure Sergeant Cobb will arrange for that along with DNA tests," Abby said.

Tamara stared at the flip phone in Abby's hand. "Do you think they'll let me have Moses back?"

"That will be up to Judge Swink." Abby wiped the smears off the screen. "I expect he'll take into consideration the fact that you've both already started working through your problems with Rev. Hale."

She handed the phone to Tamara.

"I think it would be best if you make this call yourself."

EPILOGUE

I T'S A GOOD THING WE GOT here early," Mary said as Abby helped maneuver her chair into place beside their regular pew. "This place is packed."

Indeed it was. Special events such as this dedication service usually meant a fuller church since nonmember family and friends showed up to watch the special ceremonies, but today's turnout was high even by those standards. Even William Jansen was here to report on the event for *The Birdcall.*

"Good morning," Rev. Hale said from the podium after everyone had settled in for the morning service. "First off this morning, I'd like to announce the formation of a new group, which will be led by Ellen Stanton and Terza Choi. The Empty Arms support group is for people who've suffered the loss of a family member. These two ladies know what it's like to endure such a difficult time in their lives. They saw a need in our community, so they decided to find the purpose in their own personal tragedies and begin using the experience to help and support others."

He turned and gestured toward the newspaperman sitting in the second row.

"I know this is not why you're here, but it would help to get the Empty Arms meetings off to a good start if a write-up appeared in *The Birdcall*."

William lifted his small pad and pencil to indicate he was already taking notes. "Consider it done."

In the row in front of him, Pete and Tamara waited patiently, a white-gowned bundle perched on Pete's lap. To their right, Steve Hunsicker grabbed Beau by the ankle as he attempted to crawl under the pew and carefully scooted him out. He passed the boy off to Jenny and "Aunt Charlotte," who attempted to distract him with some paper and crayons.

Next Rev. Hale called both couples and their children to the front where an open Bible rested on a podium.

Beau tried to dart in front of the Prestons. Steve scooped him up to carry him the rest of the way.

When they at last clustered around the preacher, one family on each side, Rev. Hale explained that each set of parents had come to dedicate their children's lives to godly living. By being here today, they were promising to teach them about the Bible, bring them to church regularly, and raise them according to God's commandments and biblical virtues.

He read the story of Hannah who had prayed for a child and was given Samuel, a son she dedicated to be raised in the church and who ultimately became a spiritual leader of his time.

To Rev. Hale's right, the fair haired, light skinned Prestons waited for the ceremony to begin. The baby, with his brown eyes and black hair, rested in the crook of Tamara's arm, his homemade white gown flowing down below his bootied feet.

Pete, looking like the proudest papa on earth, stood tall, his arm looped comfortably around his wife's back. Though the baby looked very little like his parents, there was no doubt that they were already a strongly knit family.

"Daniel Moses Preston," Rev. Hale said, turning toward the trio. After he asked the parents to confirm their commitment to the child, to each other, and most importantly to God, he placed his hand on the child's head and prayed aloud, asking for the Lord's blessing on this family.

Abby felt her throat tighten at the sweetness of the ceremony. She glanced at her parents, who smiled as if they were the child's actual grandparents. In a way, little Moses, hereafter to be known as Danny, would always be a part of their lives whether he lived here or on the other side of the world.

To her right was another person who took a personal interest in this dedication. After Tamara had made that call to Henry, he had personally helped the couple through every step of the process of getting the child back in their custody. He had recommended leniency from Judge Swink and offered to make unannounced visits to the Prestons' home for the duration of Tamara's probation. In addition, he also put in a good word for Pete, who was going through the process to legally adopt Danny as his son.

If anyone had doubted Pete's commitment to raising the child as his own, those doubts were dispelled when he had quit his lucrative job. To ensure that he would have plenty of time to spend with his wife and new son, he secured a job working at the Sparrow Island Medical Center.

Henry turned and smiled at Abby. "Good work," he whispered and gave her a low-five handshake.

Now Rev. Hale addressed the other family. "Beauregard Clement Hunsicker," he said, using Jenny and Steve's last name even though the adoption wouldn't be final for another few months.

Beau leaned over Steve's arm and pointed toward a satin bow that had been affixed to the end of the pew where new families had sat. "Wha's 'at?" When Rev. Hale touched his hand to the boy's head, Beau contorted his face into a delightful grimace and hammed it up for the congregation who broke into quiet ripples of laughter.

To Abby's left, Ellen stirred restlessly. Like the others, she had laughed at Beau's antics, but Abby knew that her mind was on the little boy she'd cared for during the first two weeks of his life.

"It's amazing how one tiny baby can change so many people's lives," she said leaning toward her mother. "Because of God working through him, there's the Empty Arms group, his parents are closer than ever before and now Beau has a permanent family. And they're all closer to God because of having known Danny."

Ellen leaned back against the pew and smiled contentedly. "If he can do all that in just a few short months, I can't wait to see what he'll do with the rest of his life."

A NOTE FROM THE EDITORS

THIS ORIGINAL BOOK WAS created by the Books and Inspirational Media Division of Guideposts, the world's leading inspirational publisher. Founded in 1945 by Dr. Norman Vincent Peale and his wife Ruth Stafford Peale, Guideposts helps people from all walks of life achieve their maximum personal and spiritual potential. Guideposts is committed to communicating positive, faith-filled principles for people everywhere to use in successful daily living.

Our publications include award-winning magazines like *Guideposts, Angels on Earth, Sweet 16* and *Positive Thinking*, best-selling books, and outreach services that demonstrate what can happen when faith and positive thinking are applied to day-to-day life.

For more information, visit us online at www.guideposts.org, call (800) 431-2344 or write Guideposts, 39 Seminary Hill Road, Carmel, New York 10512.